"You are going to find the right woman to love you and have your children,"

Annah told Luke, taking his hand in hers.

"I don't know. It's getting harder instead of easier. All the women I've met are so evenly matched." Her hand felt wonderful in his. He pulled it up to his cheek, to hold her there.

The rasp of his evening whiskers against the back of her hand sent a thrill racing through her. "Trust your feelings, Luke. They'll point you in the right direction."

"I don't think so," he said positively.

How could he possibly choose the right bride when all he could think about was Annah—the one woman he could never marry?

Dear Reader,

This month, Romance is chock-full of excitement. First, VIRGIN BRIDES continues with *The Bride's Second Thought*, an emotionally compelling story by bestselling author Elizabeth August. When a virginal bride-to-be finds her fiancé with another woman, she flees to the mountains for refuge...only to be stranded with a gorgeous stranger who gives her second thoughts about a lot of things....

Next, Natalie Patrick offers up a delightful BUNDLES OF JOY with *Boot Scootin' Secret Baby*. Bull rider Jacob "Cub" Goodacre returns to South Dakota for his rodeo hurrah, only to learn he's still a married man...and father to a two-year-old heart tugger. BACHELOR GULCH, Sandra Steffen's wonderful Western series, resumes with the story of an estranged couple who had wed for the sake of their child...but wonder if they can rekindle their love in *Nick's Long-Awaited Honeymoon*.

Rising star Kristin Morgan delivers a tender, sexy tale about a woman whose biological clock is booming and the best friend who consents to being her *Shotgun Groom*. If you want a humorous—red-hot!—read, try Vivian Leiber's *The 6'2", 200 lb. Challenge*. The battle of the sexes doesn't get any better! Finally, Lisa Kaye Laurel's fairy-tale series, ROYAL WEDDINGS, draws to a close with *The Irresistible Prince*, where the woman hired to find the royal a wife realizes *she* is the perfect candidate!

In May, VIRGIN BRIDES resumes with Annette Broadrick, and future months feature titles by Suzanne Carey and Judy Christenberry, among others. So keep coming back to Romance, where you're sure to find the classic tales you love, told in fresh, exciting ways.

Enjoy!

Joan Marlow Golan

Joan Marlow Golan
Senior Editor, Silhouette Romance

Please address questions and book requests to:
Silhouette Reader Service
U.S.: 3010 Walden Ave., P.O. Box 1325, Buffalo, NY 14269
Canadian: P.O. Box 609, Fort Erie, Ont. L2A 5X3

THE IRRESISTIBLE PRINCE

Lisa Kaye Laurel

Silhouette

ROMANCE™

Published by Silhouette Books

America's Publisher of Contemporary Romance

To Cindi and Chip—
for our growing-up memories
and our grown-up friendship.

 SILHOUETTE BOOKS

ISBN 0-373-19293-2

THE IRRESISTIBLE PRINCE

Copyright © 1998 by Lisa Rizoli

Printed in U.S.A.

Books by Lisa Kaye Laurel

Silhouette Romance

The Groom Maker #1107
Mommy for the Moment #1173
*The Prince's Bride #1251
*The Prince's Baby #1263
*The Irresistible Prince #1293

*Royal Weddings

LISA KAYE LAUREL

has worked in a number of fields, but says that nothing she's done compares to the challenges—and rewards—of being a full-time mom. Her extra energy is channeled into creating stories. She counts writing high on her list of blessings, which is topped by the love and support of her husband, her son, her daughter, her mother and her father.

Anders Point Gazette

PRINCE GOES UNDERCOVER TO FIND A BRIDE

Chapter One

Annah barely heard the front doorbell over the giggles and chatter of the half dozen teenagers who were prowling around her secondhand shop in search of dresses to wear to their fall formal. She was on the phone with her accountant, anyway, scribbling a note to herself to look up those figures he kept calling about while tactfully declining his offer to fix her up with his almost-divorced lawyer friend.

When she hung up, the doorbell rang again but so did the phone. It was a supplier this time, calling to break the news that the replacement part she'd ordered for her big coffeepot had been lost in transit. He was trying to track it down, but as it was now nearly five o'clock, he wouldn't be able to honor his guarantee of same-day delivery. Annah hung up the phone with a groan, knowing that there was no way she would be able to handle the morning rush in her coffee shop without that part.

A tremendous crash brought her out of her office on

the run; the teenagers had knocked over a rack of gowns. None of the girls was hurt, but the volume of talk and laughter tripled as they struggled to right the rolling rack. When the doorbell sounded for the third time, Annah seized on the excuse to escape the chaos, stepping over the pile of dresses that all but blocked the doorway. After nearly tripping in the hall, she stopped in the front room to peel away an errant sash that had wound itself around her leg. She threw it aside, and it sailed over the coffee counter and draped itself dramatically over the defunct coffeepot like a pink satin noose.

Annah rolled her eyes ceilingward and said dryly, "If you're out there, fairy godmother, this would be a real good time to blow the cobwebs off that magic wand of yours and zap me a miracle."

She flung open the door. There, looking as if he had just stepped out of the pages of a fairy tale onto her front porch, was a handsome prince.

Annah stood staring at him for a few moments, clinging to the doorknob while a frosty November wind whistled around her. Oddly enough, the strangest sensation of rising heat began to infuse her—a prickly kind of warmth that crept over her like the chills she should have been feeling in the cold air. What was happening to her? All of a sudden she was spiking a fever and hallucinating princes. Maybe she was getting the flu. Or else the afternoon from hell had been too much for her. That was it. Her imagination had finally gone haywire and sent her over the edge.

She blinked and looked again at the man standing not two feet in front of her. When she finally met his eyes, the physical jolt it gave her decided the matter: the prince on her porch was no hallucination, and no one in her right mind would call him a figment. He filled the doorway to Annah's coffee shop, regal and imposing, six feet of muscled male all packaged up in an impeccable charcoal gray suit. The wind was ruffling his hair and bringing her the faint but very real scent of a woodsy, masculine shampoo. This was no storybook prince, but a real-world ruler from a land across the ocean who came fully equipped with a royal pedigree—and the most blatant bedroom eyes Annah had ever seen on a man.

"Annah Lane?" he asked, his deep voice betraying just a hint of an accent.

"You—you know my name?" she blurted out. They had met briefly a few months earlier, at the marriage of her friend Julie to his friend Prince Erik. He had made a strong impression on her, but she never expected that he would remember an unremarkable woman who had been just one of many introductions that day. She cleared her throat. "I mean, how nice to see you again. Your Highness," she added belatedly.

He didn't smile, exactly, but his lips twitched before he spoke. "It seems that you know who I am, as well."

Shocker, she thought wryly. Any woman between the ages of eighteen and eighty who had a pulse would recognize him at a glance—even if he showed up out of the blue on her doorstep. He was Prince Lucas of the Constellation Isles, the inveterate bachelor prince whose marriage deadline had created an international furor. He had the world's most prominent women tied up in knots waiting for him to choose one of them to be his bride. Annah couldn't imagine a less likely place for him to be than here in her little out-of-the-way town on the coast of Maine.

"What brings you to Anders Point, Your Highness?'' she asked, her voice filled with its customary warmth and with newly piqued curiosity. He was friends with the Anders brothers, but no one was living at their family castle at the tip of the Point right now, what with both princes newly married and taking time off to enjoy wedded bliss.

"I've come here to see you, Miss Lane."

"Me?" Annah said incredulously. A prince looking for a bride, and he'd come this far off the beaten path just to see *her?*

"Yes. I would like to speak with you."

"Certainly," she said, her heart banging around in her chest like an empty trash can rolling down a hill. "Won't you come in?"

His glance swept the dimly lit room that housed her coffee shop and came back to rest on her again. "This is a private, personal matter," he said in a low voice that made those warm chills race along her skin.

"I...see." She gulped. "My coffee shop is closed, so we'll have privacy here."

Just then a wave of laughter swept in from the back room. He looked at her questioningly.

"Oh, I forgot. I'm waiting on a batch of customers in my secondhand shop in back. That's my other business," she explained. There was a loud shuffling noise, and one of the girls called out for her. "I'd better take care of this." Whatever was happening back there, it was something she felt more up to handling than the prince's sudden appearance in her life. A little dose of real life—her life—might not be a bad idea right now.

His eyebrows drew down in the slightest frown. "Miss Lane, this is a matter of import...and urgency."

"I figured it must be. That's why I'm going to see you next," Annah assured him. "Right after I finish with these customers and close up shop." She saw his frown deepen. Unless she missed her guess, it wasn't every day that His Highness the Prince of the Constellation Isles was asked to wait his turn while the owner of a modest secondhand shop sold used clothing to a group of teenagers. "You're welcome to come back and have a look around in the meantime," she added politely.

Just then a new gale of giggling swept in from the back room. She glanced down the hallway and then looked back at the prince. Somehow she couldn't picture him browsing through the racks with the girls. "On second thought, maybe you'd be better off waiting up front here, Your Highness. Please, come in and make yourself comfortable."

He hesitated just inside the doorway, looking about as comfortable as a snowman at the equator. A tiny, wayward impulse plucked at Annah's heart. Not caring that she was probably breaching several of the more consequential rules of royal etiquette, she took him by the arm and steered him over to the counter. He felt solid and real under the expensive material of his suit jacket, and Annah felt that unfamiliar tide of warmth begin to rise again. She dropped his arm abruptly and went behind the counter, busying herself with filling a teakettle.

"Feel free to make yourself a cup of tea. Water's on, and you'll find everything you need here behind the counter," she said as she hurried off. "I'll be back as soon as I can."

In the hallway she paused to exhale, leaning back against the wall. She addressed the ceiling again. "You know, when I asked for a miracle before, I was thinking more along the lines of the deliveryman with my replacement part. Are you sure this isn't some kind of a mistake?''

She glanced over her shoulder, but the prince didn't disappear in a puff of smoke, so she disappeared into her secondhand shop.

Prince Lucas leaned over and grasped the edge of the counter, slowly counting to ten as his knuckles turned white. Waiting was the *last* thing he wanted to do right now. Time was running short for him, shorter with each tick of the clock. A delay after he had come this far served no purpose beyond giving him fodder for second-guessing—which was all too easy to do when he was on the verge of putting his pride on the line. This was a real gamble, coming here to see this woman with whom he was barely acquainted. It wouldn't take much to send him walking back out that door before he even asked her what he had come to ask her.

He released his grip and straightened up, trying to relax by sheer force of will. He looked around him, feeling conspicuously out of place in her cozy little house in this quaint little town that time and tourists seemed to have overlooked. It was one thing to think of Annah Lane as an abstract idea. It was quite another to come barging into her world to turn that idea into a proposal.

Right now the whole idea seemed more like a foolish risk than a viable solution. And even beyond convincing himself, he had to convince *her*. Because, dammit, he needed her; he had never *needed* anyone as he needed her right now. The stakes couldn't be higher for him...and his hand was forced.

After his father's unexpected death last year, Lucas,

his only child, had assumed rule of the Constellation Isles, as tradition would have it. His succession was unanimously confirmed by a vote of the council of elders, the elected body that ruled hand in hand with the prince, but with one great big caveat. To stay on the throne, he had to get married—and he had just one year in which to do it.

On paper, a year had seemed like enough time. Not surprisingly, ever since the deadline had been announced, women had been launching themselves at him from all sides. But even in the exclusive stratum of society that was the milieu of royalty, an altar-bound prince seemed to meet nothing but social climbers, hangers-on and mercenaries—all cleverly disguised as the ideal princess. He himself had met one too many. After ten months Lucas had finally faced up to the fact that the kind of woman he wanted wouldn't be the type to come sashaying up to the palace gates, anyway. He would have to go to her. So here he was.

He paced between the counter and the window, finding a narrow path through a maze of closely set, round tables that were each bracketed by a pair of wooden chairs. Coming here had been the idea of his two closest friends. They were brothers, princes of Isle Anders, which was his country's long-time ally and closest neighbor in the remote North Atlantic waters near Iceland. Prince Erik and Prince Whit had both recently married, well and fruitfully—Whit had finally settled down with the love of his life, who was the mother of his six-year-old daughter, and Erik and his adored—and adoring—new bride were expecting a honeymoon baby to arrive in the spring. There would be no shortage of heirs to the throne in the kingdom of Isle Anders, and no shortage of marital happiness, either.

That was it in a nutshell. Lucas wanted what his friends had found. And they had both found their princesses in America: sweet, smart, down-to-earth women homegrown right here in Anders Point, Maine. So Erik and Whit had sent him to Anders Point; more specifically, they had sent him to their wives' friend, Annah Lane. Lucas had enough reservations about the whole thing to sink his island home, but it was more of a plan than he had been able to come up with, and when push came to shove, doing something was infinitely preferable to doing nothing but listen to the hourly chime of the big tower clock in the courtyard outside of his palace.

The kettle whistled softly as steam came out of its spout. He thought again of her inviting him to make himself a cup of tea, as if he should know how to do that. He wished he did. He could use a drink of any kind. But after glancing over the bewildering array of unfamiliar things behind the counter, he spun away. Pacing over to the big front window, he stared out into the dusk. In the darkness he saw her reflection as she worked in the room down the hall. Having seen her up close, he felt objectively that nothing about her looks confirmed his friends' insistence that she was an extraordinary woman. She was of medium height and medium build, with medium brown hair cut to medium length. Her eyes were uncommonly large and expressive, but they were a common enough shade of brown. Only her lips departed from the earthy hues of the rest of her coloring; they were a lush, rich red that enhanced her every expression, whether upturned with amusement or softened with empathy. But not pouty with flirtiness, which seemed to be the standard for feminine lips since he had been given his deadline. That was refreshing, at least. And for the reason he had come to her, other qualities were far more important than looks.

He turned away from the window and positioned himself in one of the creaky wooden chairs, in order to get a better view into the well-lit back room. Sounds filtered down the hallway, and what he saw and heard caught his interest. The customers she had felt obliged to wait on were no more than girls, and they were keeping her busy. One was asking her opinion as she twirled in front of a mirror in a long dress. Another wanted to look at something in a locked jewelry case. Yet another was asking to try on a hat that was on a top shelf. Many another person would have snapped and growled by now, but it seemed that nothing was too much for Annah Lane. From climbing a ladder for the hat to kneeling on the ground to pin up a hemline, she handled it all with calm efficiency. Her patience seemed unending, and that too would be a desirable trait in the person he was looking for. She always seemed to be almost smiling, as if there was some hidden well of humor within her; and when her laughter bubbled up, it sounded genuine.

As it had been during the brief time she had spoken to him, her warmth was palpable. That was what kept him there in the chair, when his better judgment was of the opinion that he should cut and run. The sounds gradually dwindled, and at last she ushered the girls out the back door and turned the latch. True to her promise, she flicked out the lights and made her way down the hall toward him.

It was too late to turn back now. Now he could only hope for the best, but be prepared for the worst—that she would say no.

* * *

Annah was uncomfortably aware of the prince's eyes
on her as she walked down the hallway. She had noticed him watching her while she was working, and had
a spot of dried blood on her finger where she had
jabbed herself with a pin to prove it. She had been a
bit unsteady on the ladder, too, as if proximity to a
prince had the power to upset her equilibrium. But Annah's calm had never been rattled by royalty before.
After all, hadn't her best friends just married princes?
But there was something about this particular prince.

He stood up as she entered the room, and Annah
found herself nearly overwhelmed by his sheer physical
presence. "Thank you for waiting," she said.

His answer was a regal incline of his head.

She glanced behind the counter and saw the kettle
gently steaming. "Oh. Didn't you have any tea?"

He seemed to hesitate a moment before answering.
"No. I...didn't."

It dawned on her then that a prince might consider
performing such a task beneath him. "Would you care
for some now?" she asked, smiling slightly.

"Yes. Thank you."

She poured a cup for each of them while he watched.
"Please, sit down," she said, placing the cups at one
of three booths that lined the far wall. He waited until
she was seated and then slid into the opposite bench.
When Annah was serving customers there, the booth
seemed like a nice roomy spot. But sitting across from
Prince Lucas, she was preoccupied with the thought
that the smallest slouch on her part would bring her
knees into contact with those of His Highness.

She sat as straight as she could, waiting for him to
say something, but he seemed more inclined to study
her. Tension wound in her like a spring, while she went

through the motions of fishing out her tea bag with a spoon. "You said you wanted to speak with me," she said, when she could stand it no longer.

"Yes."

"About whatever is troubling you?"

His eyes met hers abruptly. "Why do you say that?" he asked cautiously.

"The fact that you seemed bent on wearing a path in my linoleum was a dead giveaway," she pointed out gently.

"You are correct," he said. "I have a problem, and I am here because I have been told that you can help me, Miss Lane." His smoky voice brought an odd tinge of warmth to Annah's insides. "Prince Erik and Prince Whit of Isle Anders have both, ah—" his slight hesitation made her breath catch, in spite of herself "—recommended you."

Erik and Whit had recently married Annah's two best friends. That explained what had brought him here, but not what he wanted. "Recommended me?" she asked, frowning. "What sort of a problem is it, Your Highness?"

"In order to keep the throne, I must be married by the first of the year." He stopped, as if hoping that would be sufficient explanation.

"I know," Annah told him. "*Everyone* knows that, Your Highness." She took a sip of tea, waiting for him to elaborate on how she could help him with his wedding plans. Although amused by the thought, she refrained from asking whether he needed her to clothe the royal wedding party or to cater the reception. "What exactly is it that you need?" she asked diplomatically.

He looked deep into her eyes. "A bride," he said softly.

Annah felt her teacup slip out of her hand. It fell back onto the saucer with a crash. She ignored it, staring at him. He was in deadly earnest, of that she had no doubt. And so there it was. His softly spoken words found a home deep inside her, a place that had been waiting just for them, it seemed. He had said what she hadn't even dared let herself think, although the notion had been flickering around the edges of her mind ever since he had appeared. That was why he had come so far to see her—he wanted to make her his bride. Who would ever have believed that a fairy tale could come to life? But it was happening to her. Her handsome prince had finally come to rescue her, and now all of the dreams that she had thought impossible were going to come true at last. She sat there overcome, unable to speak.

"Will you do it, Miss Lane?" he asked then. "Will you help find me a bride?"

Annah stared at him. *Find* him a bride? Not *be* his bride? A cloud of confusion swept over her, but the direct look he gave her on the heels of his direct question dispelled it like a brisk wind. *Find* him a bride. His words tolled the death knell of her reawakening dreams. She looked away quickly. Of course he hadn't meant that he wanted to marry her, she chided herself. Not her, Annah Lane. How quickly her fancies had allowed her to forget that she wasn't at all the kind of woman that a man would want for a wife, to have and to hold, for better…for worse. Annah took a deep breath, and the pungent scents of coffee beans and dish detergent in her shop provided a strong dose of reality. No prince was going to come walking through that door to marry her. Fairy tales had to have a happily ever after, and her life was no fairy tale.

However, her life did have a prince in it, for the moment at least. He was watching her, waiting for an answer to his question. He didn't want her to be his princess, but he did want her to be his... *matchmaker?*

Looking at him, Annah found it hard to believe that the man sitting across from her needed anyone's help in finding a bride. True, the matrimonial clock was ticking for him; but he was arguably the most eligible bachelor in the world. He was rich, handsome—and he was a *prince,* for gosh sakes! International scuttlebutt had it that he was putting off choosing a bride until he had made the most of his last few months of bachelorhood, and Annah had never doubted that. There were legions of women stalking him: famous women, beautiful women—princess wanna-bes who would gladly trade their names and whatever virtue they could claim for the allure, luxury and power of a regal lifestyle. If he wanted to get married to save his throne, all he had to do was turn around and let himself be caught by one of them. Unless...

She looked at him carefully. He was staring out of the window now, his mouth set in a grim line. Suddenly she understood why Erik and Whit had sent him to her, of all people. "Your Highness, you want more than just a bride for the throne, don't you?" she said softly.

"Yes," he said, giving her a direct gaze. "I want more."

Annah sat back in her seat in the booth. *Now* it all made sense. The gossip had been wrong, and so had she. He had delayed choosing a bride not to enjoy the countdown of his bachelor days, but for the simple reason that he hadn't found the right woman. And the friends who had nudged him her way knew about her "gift"—her mysterious insight for recognizing true love. On paper, that made her the ideal matchmaker.

How was she supposed to answer him? Her insight wasn't exactly something she could control, or even understand. It might not even work for him. She looked at him then, really looked at him, and a smoky feminine awareness caressed her insides in a curl of warmth. It had nothing to do with his being a prince, and everything to do with her reaction to him on a far more elemental level. In his mid-thirties, he carried himself with the unselfconscious assurance of a fully mature man. The power she had sensed within him was manifest in his rugged build. His touch-me brown hair and the well-trimmed beard that matched it rippled with mahogany. And deep in those sensual gray eyes lived an intensity that was compelling. His inner vibrations were strong, but that didn't mean they'd be easy to read. Again those warm chills passed over her body, unbidden and mysterious.

She excused herself and got up from the booth, fanning herself with her hand. In the hallway, she checked the thermostat to see if it had been accidentally bumped up by one of the girls, but it was at the usual setting. Seeking solace in the familiar, she busied herself getting a rag from behind the counter and wiping the tea she had spilled. Then she righted her cup and refilled it.

What could Lucas do, except wait for her answer? He gritted his teeth, feeling his patience stretch thin. And it wasn't just the waiting. Everything about this situation went against the grain. It was hard enough for a man like him to have to ask for anything, but this—*this* was an insult to his masculinity. What kind of a man needed help in finding his own bride?

A man who had played with fire and gotten himself burned, that's what kind. Only a fool would be anything but careful after that. Lucas would be very, *very* careful.

Still, as hellish as the wedding deadline had made his life, Lucas had to applaud the decision of the council of elders. His marrying was in the best interest of the country he loved, which had a long history as a representative monarchy. As its prince, he had a duty to preserve the succession and carry that history into the future. He had to provide heirs to the throne. Marriage was inevitable. But the *deadline* had been a stroke of genius, focusing the attention of the world on his little country—and on its finely crafted jewelry, unique scenery and old-world hospitality. Yes, the elders had their eyes nobly focused on the past and the future—and their fingers wisely wrapped around the present, tightly gripping the collective pocketbook of the Constellation Isles. Tourism had swelled, even during the off-season. You had to love that. And the deadline served another purpose. Although none knew why, the elders were wise enough to see that, at thirty-five, their prince needed a little push toward the altar. He could still feel their fingers in his back, all the way across the ocean.

Annah returned to her seat. "Is the tea all right, Your Highness?" she asked him, gesturing toward his untouched cup.

He looked at it as if just now noticing its existence. "Yes. It's fine, thank you," he said, and concentrated on taking a drink. She could feel the tension in him.

Annah was a toucher. She felt the strongest impulse

to reach out and pat him on the arm, but an even stronger instinct told her that he wouldn't appreciate that kind of reassurance. And in truth she didn't know how well she could handle her own reaction if she laid a hand on him again. "You…you've taken me a little by surprise," she said truthfully. "I'm not sure what to say."

A look flickered across his face, almost of pain. "There is some irony, is there not, in a prince having to ask for help in such a matter?" he said, with a twist of his mouth that passed for a smile. "But being a prince does not make me an expert in this area, Miss Lane."

His lack of confidence in matters of the heart was typically male, and thoroughly endearing. Just talking about it was costing him, that much was obvious. But she was no expert herself!

He went on. "I have only one chance, and precious little time. I don't want to make a mistake that I will pay for the rest of my life."

"No, of course not." Annah thought that was an odd way of putting it. Not wanting to choose the wrong woman, instead of wanting to choose the right woman.

"That's why I am willing to put myself—my future—into your hands. Miss Lane, with or without your help, I will be married in two months. That is a fact of my life, because of a circumstance that I cannot change." He paused. "But whether I will be happily married depends upon whether or not you will help me."

She knew—oh, did she ever know!—that there was only one way he would be happy in marriage, and that was if he found true love. Without knowing why, she sensed somehow that behind his wariness, beneath his jaded exterior, that was what he was really looking for, whether or not he knew it or wanted to admit it. But she of all people knew that love was a tricky thing. She could match him up with every woman in town and see true love if it was there—but if it wasn't, she couldn't conjure it out of thin air. She bit her lip, stymied. How could she explain that to him?

He seemed to take her silence as discouragement. She could almost feel him pluck up his courage before he made one last appeal. "Miss Lane, I need your help," he said, his voice resonant with feeling. "If not for my sake, then for the sake of the children I am depending upon this marriage to give me."

Children. He not only wanted a happy marriage, but he wanted children, too. The undisguised hunger in his voice set off a vibration of longing deep inside Annah, a feeling whose strength surprised her, given how long it had been since she had last allowed herself to indulge in it. Once upon a time, she too had wanted it all.

He lowered his voice to a raw whisper. "Please don't refuse me."

She swallowed once, painfully, and put the errant memory back in its place. Then she looked up, and their eyes caught and held. It was as if she were looking into the deep shadows of those gray eyes for the first time, her vision untainted by preconceived notions of who he was or what he wanted. Something in that silent exchange made Annah feel as though a match had been struck somewhere deep inside her, and the flame had caught hold in her innermost self.

No, it couldn't be—no—it must be empathy that had engendered this sudden bond. For who better than she could understand the yearning and the uncertainty in his gaze? The prince was chasing a dream, an oh-so-beautiful fairy tale. It had eluded Annah, but it could come true for him. The growing warmth inside her seemed to fire her very being. In that moment of shared romantic hope, all her reservations turned to ash. Far from refusing his request, she knew she would move heaven and earth and Anders Point itself, rock by rock, in order to help him.

He needed his dream to come true. And if he had the will, she just might have the way.

Chapter Two

Prince Lucas had started pacing again by the time the huge grandfather clock in the castle entry hall chimed quarter to eight. The relief he had felt when Annah Lane had told him that she would help him had faded in the few hours since he had left her house and come here to the castle at the tip of the Point. While he had slept off the worst of his jet lag, showered and dressed for dinner, a renewed sense of urgency had crept back in.

He had wanted to talk strategy immediately, but she had suggested that they do it over dinner. Even that slight delay in getting the process rolling was frustrating for him, but then, he had been hashing all this over for ten months. It made sense to give her a few hours to do the same.

The sound of his echoing footsteps received the sudden punctuation of a ring at the front doorbell. He swung open the heavy front door. "Good evening, Miss Lane," he greeted her.

"Good evening, Your Highness," she answered. She was carrying a large, two-handled pot, which she set down on an antique table in the entry hall.

"What's that?" he asked, looking puzzled.

"Dinner," she said succinctly. She disappeared out the door again, heading for the car that was parked in the front drive, and fished a couple of large paper bags out of the trunk.

"Did you *make* dinner?" he asked when she returned.

"Of course," she said, sounding surprised at his surprise. "I told you I would."

He had assumed that her offer to "take care of dinner" meant that she was going to order the meal from a restaurant and arrange for its delivery. "You shouldn't have gone to such trouble."

"It's no trouble," she said, smiling as if that were true while she breezed past him. "Grab that pot for me, would you?" she called over her shoulder.

What could he do? He picked up the pot and carried it obediently into the kitchen.

"Just set it on one of the back burners," she said as she put the bags on the counter. If her voice sounded breathy, she hoped he would think it was from lugging dinner up the stone steps out front. The truth was that she had once more been thrown off balance simply by being near him, although she wasn't sure why. A woman who was nearly thirty ought to be able to be in the presence of a handsome prince without having her backbone begin to melt. That she had never felt this way around Prince Erik or Prince Whit must be because they were "hometown" princes. Their mother had been from Anders Point, and the two of them were no strangers to the town when they stayed here in their family's castle.

If she felt differently around Prince Lucas, she would just have to get over it. She reminded herself of the deep bond she had felt between them before he had left her coffee shop. Making his dream come true was what mattered. And if she was going to help him, she couldn't be walking on eggshells around him just because he was royalty. Not if her plan was going to work.

She was starting to struggle out of her jacket when his voice came from close behind her, soft and low. "Allow me."

She kept her back to him while he helped her off with her jacket, chiding herself for her weak-kneed reaction to his performing this small courtesy for her. While he left the room with it, she busied herself getting dinner underway. "I have a few things to finish up," she told him when he returned.

He had that slight frown that she was becoming familiar with. "What with preparing this meal, Miss Lane, have you had any time to think about my situation?"

He was direct, she had to give him that. She looked up from the pot she was stirring. "I do my best thinking when I'm cooking," she told him with a smile.

"Then by all means, cook," he said briskly. He stood next to her at the counter, which had the effect of totally disrupting her thinking. It was just the feel of his nearness, because she had to look out of the corner of her eye to see him—not that she was sure that was a great idea, either. He had been born a prince...did he have to be so darned attractive, too? The man was a walking woman-magnet even without a wedding deadline, and Annah could well imagine the world's social climbers climbing all over each other to get at him. There weren't women like that here in Anders Point, but even here they would act differently around him, less comfortably, knowing he was a prince. That was just human nature. Annah knew her plan was right on target. But she wasn't about to just blurt it out. She had a feeling it would be better to get him used to the idea gradually.

"Nice castle, isn't it?" she asked conversationally.

"Yes," he answered. "It is not large, but it is beautifully sited up here on this bluff."

"As a place used only for their stays in America, I suppose the Anders family didn't need it to be large. And it will be plenty big enough for Whit and Drew to live in after they return from their honeymoon. Lexi is thrilled about moving in here."

He seemed to smile slightly at the mention of his friend's six-year-old daughter, but merely said, "I was glad of Whit's offer to let me stay here while I am in town."

That was the opening Annah was looking for. He wouldn't be staying in the castle long, if she had her way. "By the way, no one else knows you're here, do they?"

He seemed a bit surprised by her change of subject, but answered her question. "Besides the Anders family? No one except you…and my staff, of course."

"But no one here in town," she clarified. "I mean, it was dark when you left my place, and you drove away in a nondescript sedan."

He nodded. His chauffeur, who was also his bodyguard, insisted on it, for security reasons. He only used a limo for public occasions.

"After that, did you come right here to the castle?"

"Yes."

"Did anyone walk by while you were on my porch?"

He gave her a puzzled look. "I didn't notice anyone."

"And I know the girls I was waiting on didn't really get a good look at you," she said positively. "So you see, I am the only one in town who knows that you—that Prince Lucas of the Constellation Isles is here."

His frown deepened. "You think that's important?"

"Of course," she said. As an afterthought she added, "Don't you?"

He didn't. Wasn't she aware that once other people saw him, they would recognize him? He expected that. It went with the territory.

Her question dangled intriguingly. He didn't answer, and she didn't elaborate, but turned her attention to the food. "The salad is all ready now, so I'll just slice up the bread."

Lucas stood aside, watching her. "When I asked you to dinner, I had no intention of your cooking and serving it," he said.

"I enjoy cooking," she said, putting the bread into a basket that she had pulled out of one of the upper cabinets. "Anyway, I've been thinking of expanding my coffee shop hours and serving lunch, also. It's nice having a guinea pig to try out my new recipes."

No one had ever had the cheek to refer to him as a guinea pig before, and oddly enough, Lucas found he didn't mind. But it still felt awkward, having his guest prepare her own dinner. Standing out of her way as she bustled about, he observed, "You seem to be familiar with this kitchen."

"Julie lived here as the caretaker for a year before she married Prince Erik," she said, pulling a bunch of flowers out of one of the bags. "She and I are friends."

Which apparently gave them intimate knowledge of each other's kitchens. He was not wise in the ways of feminine friendships, but found himself admiring the feminine grace of her movements as she worked. Bending under one counter she picked out some sort of glass container and, with a few deft moves, began arranging the flowers in it. She placed the bloom-filled bowl in the center of the big wooden trestle table that stood in front of the fireplace. Lucas watched as the drawers and cabinets that were a dark mystery to him yielded placemats, utensils, crockery and glasses at her touch. She began setting them out on the table. It looked as if she meant for the two of them to eat dinner right there.

He cleared his throat. "It was my intention that we eat in the dining room, Miss Lane."

"We don't have to be so formal. Please, call me Annah."

"And expect to dine with you here in the kitchen?" He hadn't forgotten that she was his *guest,* despite the fact that she had come in and taken charge of the meal.

But that seemed to be her preference. "It's cozier in here," she said reasonably, stirring the pot on the stove again.

"Would be, if someone had built a fire in that hearth," Lucas muttered, and then busied himself doing just that. Until now it had escaped his notice that the sweater she was wearing didn't look anywhere near as warm as his—although she filled it out a lot better, a fact which hadn't escaped his notice at all. He forced himself to concentrate on the work at hand, and soon a roaring blaze filled the big stone fireplace.

She paused in her work to look at his. "You're quite good at that," she remarked.

Lucas turned to her. "It's a skill a man learns early, where I'm from."

A hint of amusement played at the corners of her lips. "Even when you're a prince?"

"Of course," he said seriously, not sure what she was getting at. As the only child of royal parentage, he didn't have much experience with being teased. Was that what she was doing, or did she really think that his being a prince meant that he was some kind of wimp? Despite that niggling question, he found that putting his hands to use had righted his perspective. This wasn't a formal affair of state, after all, and having Annah prepare dinner seemed like much less of a big deal than the leap of faith he was taking by putting his future into her hands. Still, Lucas trusted his friends. And it was clear that he himself had no way, mysterious or otherwise, to tell whether a woman was right for him. What's more, he was wise enough to know that he needed a partner, someone who lived in the town and knew its people. Someone who could weed out the unsuitables and make introductions. Had they known about it, the grandmothers who gathered to gossip in village stores on the Constellation Isles would say that their prince had hired himself a matchmaker—and about time, too! He himself was more comfortable thinking of Annah Lane in terms of a consultant.

That thought renewed his sense of purpose and his curiosity about her qualifications. Weren't matchmakers supposed to be older, more-experienced women? "If I may be so bold as to ask, how can you help others find suitable matches when you are not married yourself?" he asked her.

"Been there, done that," she said offhandedly.

"I beg your pardon?"

"I'm divorced," she clarified.

He didn't remember Erik or Whit mentioning that. "I'm sorry," he said, feeling badly that he'd asked.

She waved away his apology. "It doesn't matter," she said. And she sounded as if it didn't.

That made him feel a little better, so he asked something that did matter. "Do you really think you'll be able to help me find the kind of woman I'm looking for?"

She seemed to be thinking it over. "Let me make sure I understand exactly what you want," she said. "First of all, why Anders Point?"

"Princes find brides here," he said, making it sound, to Annah's amusement, as if finding the right woman was a simple matter of geography. "And this seems like a pretty good place to find the kind of woman I am looking for. Someone like the women Erik and Whit found."

"Sorry," Annah said, unable to keep from smiling at that. "I'm fresh out of best friends, and even if I had one left, I don't think I'd let you have her, anyway. It's getting lonely around here, with princes swooping in and carrying them off to live happily ever after."

She hoped she wasn't imagining the slight smile she saw underneath his beard. If he had even a smidgen of a sense of humor behind that royal demeanor, maybe he would go for her plan after all. "What is it about them that you would want in a wife?" she prodded.

He thought about that. "I guess it's that they're so—" he paused, as if groping for the right word "—ordinary."

"Oh, boy," she said playfully, rolling her eyes. "You'd best keep that one under your crown, Your Highness. No woman likes to think of herself as ordinary."

"You misunderstand me," he said, frowning.

"Then make me understand," she said, smiling at him encouragingly. "If you want me to find a bride for you, give me something to work with." She placed her hand on his and jiggled it playfully, hoping to get him to lighten up a little. The casual touch had the opposite effect on her. Once again chills danced through her, and they didn't stop at the point of contact, but radiated up her arm, warm and mysterious. Again she pulled back abruptly.

If he noticed anything, she couldn't tell from his response. "When I say I want an ordinary woman, I mean a woman who's not like—" He stopped cold.

"Not like the women you meet at diplomatic parties, state dinners and other official events?" she suggested.

"That's right," he said, as if marveling at her insight.

It was as she had expected, but she was still relieved to hear him admit it. "Good," she said. "Because that's the whole basis of my plan."

"What plan?"

She took a deep breath and plunged right in. "It's simple, really," she said. "The best way to find an ordinary woman is to be an ordinary man."

"No doubt," he said dryly. "But the fact of the matter is, I am a prince."

She held her gaze steady. "You know that, and I

know that—but we've established the fact that no one else in Anders Point knows that.''

"That still doesn't make me an ordinary man," he said.

"Doesn't it?"

"Miss Lane," he began, the intensity in his gray eyes sending warmth her way.

"Annah," she said, correcting him automatically. He was an ordinary man, she told herself, and she was going to treat him like one. Not like a prince. Not like a man who could make her insides cook at a glance. Just an ordinary man.

"Annah, what exactly are you getting at?"

She looked straight at him. "Okay, here it is. I think you should go undercover."

He stared at her. "Undercover?" he repeated.

"Yes."

"You can't be serious," he said, frowning.

"Why not?" she said. "Remember, no one knows you're here."

"So you want me to change my identity?"

"Not change it—hide it," she corrected. "Your princely identity, that is."

"That's crazy!"

"On the contrary, it's perfectly logical, Your Highness," she countered calmly. "I'm not asking you to renounce the throne or anything. Just to do without your title for a while. Tell me, do you have a surname? I've only ever heard you referred to as Prince Lucas."

He was still looking at her as if she had taken leave of her good sense. "It's Hansson. By custom it is not used."

"Good," she said. "You can be here as Luke Hansson, ordinary man, instead of as Prince Lucas, ruler of the Constellation Isles and wife hunter.''

''But being a prince is who I am,'' he pointed out.

''A *part* of who you are. You're also a man, a man who says he's looking for an ordinary, small-town woman. I say she'll be easier to find if you get rid of the trappings of royalty.''

''But—''

''Trust me, your odds of success will greatly increase. It will scare off the prince groupies, and it will ensure that women act like themselves around you.''

He thought about that. Bizarre as it seemed, what she was saying made sense. Personal experience confirmed that when it came to marrying a prince, a woman would say or do or promise or pretend just about anything.

''Doing it this way will also save time,'' she added. ''It will allow us to dispense with a lot of formalities. That deadline of yours is awfully tight.''

Didn't he know it. That was the kicker. ''I'll have to think about it,'' he heard himself say.

He went down the steps to the wine cellar. What was he saying? Think about it! His intellect told him he'd have to be insane even to consider it. But the lesson he'd learned the hard way told him otherwise.

He was still thinking when he returned to the kitchen with the bottle he had chosen. Glad to have something to do with his hands, he opened it up and filled two glasses. Annah turned around from the stove as he carried them over, her cheeks flushed from cooking, and for a moment he felt an odd thrill of warmth that he couldn't quite attribute to the fire.

''Dinner is—''

''Something smells—''

They both stopped and smiled at each other. Even that slight stretching of his cheeks under his beard felt unfamiliar, making him realize how little he had done that lately.

"Delicious," he finished.

"Want to see whether it tastes as good as it smells?" she asked, holding up a spoonful of some kind of stew to his lips. He was genuinely taken aback. None of the chefs on his staff would ever dream of taking such an outrageous liberty with him, even if he had given them the opportunity by being in the kitchen. When he opened his mouth to demur, she popped the spoon inside.

He had commanded his own utensils since he had first been able. The last time anyone had spoon-fed him anything was far beyond his memory. He was her captive, standing there with a wineglass in each hand. A sensual shiver ran through him as she pulled the spoon back out, slowly, as if the better to let him savor the taste of the food. It tasted like a spoonful of heaven—with a generous helping of the fires of hell thrown in.

With a forbearance that was second nature to him, he handed her a glass of wine and lifted his own in salute. While she returned the gesture and took a sip, he took a healthy swig of his.

She noticed. "Uh-oh. Is the chili too spicy?" she asked.

"Not at all," he said, which would have been the polite response that a formal dinner guest who had the audacity to ask such a question would have gotten from him. But to her he added, "Not if one had been forewarned that it *was* chili."

Her eyes and mouth went round. "I'm so sorry! I

thought you knew. No wonder you looked…taken by surprise.''

Too much about this woman surprised him, Lucas decided as they took their seats at the big table. He had met people the world over, from all walks of life, but he had never met anyone quite like her before.

"Want some shredded cheese to go with that chili?" she asked him, interrupting his thoughts.

He looked down at the steaming bowl that she had placed on the table in front of him. "Yes, thank you," he said. She passed the cheese to him and started in on her salad, looking as if enjoying this meal was the only thing she had on her mind.

His mind was on other things, but he did notice when her glass was empty. Remembering that he was the host, he poured for her and asked, "Is there anything else you want?"

"As a matter of fact, yes. I want to know how you like the chili," she said, gesturing toward the food that he had forgotten. In the flickering light of the fire, he saw that a teasing smile played across those luscious lips of hers. "I really do. It's a new recipe."

"And I'm your guinea pig," he said dryly. He took a spoonful of chili, ready for the bite this time. He took his time chewing and swallowing, aware that she was looking at him expectantly. It was good—rich and flavorful. "I like it," he said.

She seemed pleased. "So the recipe's a keeper?" she asked.

He nodded.

"I think so, too. Chili is bound to be a big seller at lunchtime, especially this time of year."

He turned his attention back to his chili. It really did have just the right amount of oomph. He preferred it to most of the dainty delicacies that the palace chefs served. It was hot and hearty, a real man's dish. If Annah served this up along with her sweet smile at lunchtime, her tiny little coffee shop would be packed.

As if on cue, she took his empty bowl away, ladled it full and set it down in front of him again. He looked down at it, then back at her. "I didn't ask for a refill."

"I know," she said with a smile. "But you wanted one, didn't you?"

"How did you know?" he asked, starting to dig in. "Do all of us ordinary guys want seconds?"

Annah laughed. She toyed with the stem of her wineglass while he finished eating. "It's nice to know you have a sense of humor, Your Highness," she said. "It will come in handy for my plan."

"I haven't agreed to it yet."

"Well, while you're thinking about it, why don't you give me a little better idea of what you're looking for in a bride?"

Fair enough. And very simple. "I'm looking for compatibility," he said. "I want a woman I have enough in common with to share my life with, someone who wants what I want."

"Go on," Annah said encouragingly, pleased at how he was opening up. As he talked, the bond that she had first felt that afternoon seemed to strengthen. "Is there anything specific that is important to you?"

He answered without hesitation. "Above all, she has to love children and want to have them."

Annah felt each word fall on her heart like a hammer stroke. Reminding herself that she had asked for this by getting involved didn't soften the blows.

At her silence he went on to clarify. "I'm not talking about procreating to fulfill the duty of providing heirs for the succession to the throne. What I really want is a woman who will be a good and loving mother to our children,'' he said softly. ''That's the most important thing of all.''

Lucas looked away abruptly, this unaccustomed confession leaving him feeling as if he had just run a marathon. He took a sip of wine and steeled himself for more, but surprisingly she didn't follow up with another question. He looked over, only to see her gazing into the fire, looking stricken. He wondered what was wrong with his answer.

Trying not to sound defensive, he said, ''I don't see why this should be a problem.'' *Again,* he thought, frowning. ''I thought women were supposed to *want* to have children.''

She pulled her gaze back to him, but her smile looked forced. ''Most do,'' she said, her voice oddly strained.

Something about the way she said it made him ask, ''Don't you?''

''Me? I...uh—'' She shrugged. ''Babies aren't my thing.''

That explained her strange reaction. But it surprised him, given what he had seen of her. A small-town, matchmaking girl with a warm smile and a talent for dispensing cheer, hope and nourishment seemed like the maternal type to him. But then again, why should he be surprised that he had misread her so thoroughly? If he had been good at spotting that sort of thing he wouldn't be in this predicament.

Not every woman wanted babies; that concept had long been a fact of his life. The ones that didn't had their reasons. He didn't care to ask what hers were, but he supposed Annah was more interested in her businesses. As strong as the issue was for him, he was fair-minded enough to see that she could still help him, despite her personal preferences on that matter. He just wanted to be sure that she understood his. He leaned his hands on the kitchen table. "The woman I'm looking for, babies will most definitely be her 'thing,'" he said flatly.

She nodded.

"And if I have to go undercover to find her..."

She looked up at him. "You'll go along with my plan, then?"

"First tell me precisely what you have in mind."

"Okay," she said briskly. "First of all we'd have to get you out of this castle, the sooner the better. An ordinary guy would have no reason to live here."

"True. Are there any hotels in town?"

"A couple of bed-and-breakfasts, but they're closed this time of year. Besides, if you want a hometown girl, you have to be a hometown guy. You can stay at my house," she offered.

"I beg your pardon?"

"I think you should move in with me."

She sounded so casual about it! He knew what an invitation like that meant in his homeland—if he slept one night under the same roof as a single woman, they'd be married by morning! He knew what an invitation like that meant from a jaded veteran of the ultrachic international circles, too. But he had no idea in the world it meant from a woman like her, in a place like Anders Point. "Move in with you?" he repeated.

"It's perfectly logical. It will make it easier for us to work together, and I've got a spare bedroom you can have all to yourself."

Sleeping arrangements aside, he couldn't imagine

two people living in that little dollhouse of hers—in the space that wasn't taken up by her two businesses. Even this castle seemed small compared to his palace in the Constellation Isles. "I couldn't possibly impose like that," he said.

"Nonsense," she said. "I want you to."

Strange as it sounded, he believed her, and realized that he had just found out for himself what people meant when they talked about American hospitality.

"Your staying with me would also give us a reason for you to be in town," she went on. "We'll pass you off as Luke Hansson, an old friend of mine, while I get you together with women around here."

He still wasn't convinced it would be that easy. "Even with a different name, won't I be recognizable?"

She had an answer for that, too. "You would be, if we didn't change your appearance."

"Change my appearance? How?"

"There's only one way that a face that appears with such regularity on newsstands the world over is going to gain any kind of anonymity, even in a place like Anders Point," she said seriously. "And I don't think you're going to like it."

Neither did he, whatever it was. "What is it?" he asked cautiously.

"Well, the way I see it, the one thing that would work is if you get rid of your most recognizable feature. Your trademark."

He leaned his forearms on the table. "Miss Lane—"

"Annah."

"Are you suggesting that I *shave* my *beard?*"

"Oh no, I'm more than suggesting. I'm insisting."

He pushed his chair back from the table. "Unthinkable," he said with finality.

She crossed her arms. "If you don't, you'll never get away with this. Especially around women."

"No."

The word hung in the air between them for several minutes, while they faced off. "Then you'll just have to come up with another plan on your own," she said finally. "This is the only plan I have, and the only way it will work."

Getting up from the table, he put another log on the fire and watched as the flames engulfed it. He lingered there long after he needed to for the sake of fire building, thinking about what she had said.

Annah watched the flickering light play across his brooding features while she cleared the table and stacked the dishes in the dishwasher. She was tempted to break the silence, but there was really nothing more to say. It was up to him now.

When she was finished, she could see that he was still weighing her plan in his mind. "I'll tell you what," she said. "I'm going home now, so you can finish thinking this over. But you need to make a decision tonight."

"Why is that?"

"Because the castle is supposed to be empty." Whit and Drew were honeymooning, and the caretaker was on vacation. "I can explain away the lights here this evening, because I've got a set of keys and a strong need to borrow an industrial-size coffeepot," she said. "But if you're here in the morning, the jig is up. You'll be Prince Lucas, princess hunting in Anders Point."

He registered that without a word, then disappeared while she was packing up her bags. A few minutes later, he came back with her jacket. He helped her put it on, then carried the big coffee urn for her.

Outside, her car was running. She looked at him.

"I thought I'd get it warmed up for you," he said.

She found herself speechless at his thoughtfulness. He must have noticed her putting the keys in her jacket pocket when she arrived.

He opened the door for her. "Get in," he said gruffly. "You must be freezing out here."

No one was ever that concerned with her comfort. Obediently she slid behind the wheel, and he closed the door behind her. When he was halfway up the steps again, she rolled down the window. "Luke," she called out softly. He stopped for a moment before turning around and coming back to the car.

"What is it?"

He was leaning over, his face right next to hers. Another wave of warmth washed over her, in defiance of the weather. "I really think this will work," she said. "I'll keep the back door unlocked for you. Your bedroom is the one at the top of the stairs."

Chapter Three

His Highness, Prince Lucas of the Constellation Isles wiped off a corner of the steamed-up mirror in Annah's tiny bathroom and glared at his reflection. All of a sudden this hot idea was looking mighty lukewarm. He turned away from the mirror, stripped down and got into the shower.

The steamy water sluicing over him washed away his temporary misgivings. Late last night he had gone to bed feeling optimistic for the first time since he had been handed a wedding deadline. He was a man of action, and it had gone against the grain to waste ten months spinning his wheels on the slick, dating fast track. Now, thanks to Annah, he finally had a game plan, a strategy that was going to help him find the right woman to be his bride. With her plan she had given him a changed identity, a place to stay and something more. Something less tangible but far more important—hope.

He was overwhelmed by her willingness to help him,

which even extended to welcoming him into her home.
However else he felt about it, there was no doubt that
his being Annah's houseguest was the perfect cover.
Even if someone thought they recognized him, they
would discount entirely the possibility it could really
be he. Why would a prince do such a thing? Somehow
it gave him a real lift, knowing that he was anonymous
for a change. He had sent his bodyguard away, reason-
ing that if he wasn't going to be a prince, he didn't
need one. This was an adventure. What man wouldn't
thrill to the chance of going undercover? And there
would be absolutely no danger of a woman falling for
him—or pretending to fall for him—because he was a
prince.

Only Annah knew. But she was his partner, not a
potential bride, and he was glad to have her on his side.
He owed Whit and Erik for sending him to her. Not
only was she helping him, the fact was he liked Annah;
though at times he didn't understand her at all, and at
others it seemed as if there was enough friction between them to start a fire. She loved to tease him, too,
and funny thing was he didn't really mind it. Maybe
because she had plenty of sugar to go with her spice.

But even Annah couldn't sugarcoat this, he thought,
when he came out of the shower and faced the mirror
again. Thanks to her, the major part of his beard was
lying in the trash can, instead of being on his face
where it belonged, the badge of manhood he had worn
proudly since he was first able to grow it. He had
hacked it off with a ridiculously tiny pair of scissors
he had found in the medicine cabinet, one of those
fearsome, feminine instruments women did God knows
what with. As a result, he looked like he had fallen into
the clutches of a demented barber—but he knew he

would have been demented himself to try to shave his thick beard without thinning it a little first. Now, with his face warm and wet from the steamy shower, he could take the final step.

He slathered shaving cream across the remnants of his beard, making it look as if he had a white one. With razor in hand, he paused. He had realized Annah was right about his recognizability, but this was no easy task. Where he was from, the pulse of life was driven by the elements, and the elements were harsh. On the icy shores of the Constellation Isles, a man was not a man without a beard. But this would only be temporary, and for the sake of his future and the homeland he loved, it was not too great a sacrifice. Keeping his hand steady, he made the first stroke down his cheek.

Two new razor blades later, he ducked down over the sink to splash away the last of the lather clinging to his face. Burying his face in a towel, he dried it and then looked in the mirror again. His transformation was complete. Bearded Prince Lucas, ruler of the Constellation Isles, was gone. In his place stood Luke Hansson.

Luke. She had called him that last night, and it had brought him up short. He had never had a nickname before, but he liked the way it had sounded when she said it. Now, looking at a reflection of himself that he had never seen before, he felt like Luke. But it was tough to be objective about what he saw. He ran a hand across his clean-shaven face. It wouldn't send women running in the other direction. At least, he didn't think so.

There was only one way to find out for sure. He would get dressed and go downstairs, because there was one person who would not scruple to be completely honest with him. Her opinion as a consultant was invaluable. Besides that, he very much wanted to see her reaction to him—and those expressive brown eyes of hers would show him that, plain as day.

Annah was just finishing her morning cleanup in the coffee shop when the phone rang.

"Did I catch you at a good time?"

"Julie! It's always a good time to talk to you," Annah said, knowing that her friend was referring to the precious time after she closed the coffee shop and before she opened the secondhand shop. "What's new on Isle Anders?" Julie had moved there after her marriage to Prince Erik that summer.

"Not as much as is new in Anders Point."

"You're referring to?"

"Your new career, Annah."

"Oh, come on. I told you before that I was thinking about serving lunch." She finished polishing up the big coffeepot from the castle that was keeping her in business until the missing part for hers showed up.

"I'm talking about what you're doing for Prince Lucas."

Annah moved over to wipe the counter. "Oh, that."

"Yes, that! Since when are you a *matchmaker?*" Julie said teasingly.

"Since your husband and his brother sent me a client," Annah returned, giving the counter a final swipe.

"Erik talked to him this morning. I can't believe you talked him into going undercover."

"Me neither." Annah hadn't seen Luke since she'd left the castle, but late last night, after she'd gone to bed, she had heard him come in her back door. This morning when she got up to open up the coffee shop, the door to her spare bedroom was closed. She didn't know what had made up his mind, but she knew that his being here meant that he had agreed to her plan.

"Have you decided who to fix him up with yet?"

"I've got a mental list of 'possibles.'"

"Are *you* on it?" Julie asked. "I always thought there must be a prince somewhere for you, too. Maybe he's the one."

A short laugh was Annah's only answer.

"It wouldn't hurt you to give it a try. You're single. And you like him, don't you?"

Annah wasn't sure how to respond to that. It seemed so irrelevant. *Like* him? All she knew was that she turned into a human barbecue whenever she was near him. "Moot point," she told her friend. "We've already established the fact that I am out of the running." She didn't see the need to tell her friend the reason— that she didn't meet his requirement—and Julie didn't ask. Just in case, Annah changed the subject. "How is Princess Lexi doing?"

"Still wearing a cowgirl hat and boots everywhere she goes. You should see Erik giving her horsie rides—he loves being an uncle. We're having so much fun with her while her mom and dad are on their honeymoon, I wouldn't care if Drew and Whit went around the world twice." She yawned.

Annah smiled. "Is Lexi tiring you out, or is your new husband?"

"Both."

"But not as much as the next heir to the throne, I'll bet."

Annah could hear Julie's smile in her soft words. "You're right. I haven't been sleeping very well, and my stomach's all queasy."

"Morning sickness?"

"No. Excitement." Julie paused and lowered her voice. "Annah, I felt the baby move for the first time yesterday."

Annah spoke with the same tone of awe. "Oh, Julie! What did it feel like?" She couldn't help asking, even knowing it was a far-from-subtle form of self-torture. She had asked Drew that, too, when she was pregnant with Lexi, but had never gotten a satisfactory answer.

"It's—well, it simply defies description," Julie breathed. "It's something that you have to feel for yourself."

Knowing that she never would, Annah didn't know how to give her friend a direct reply without raining on her happiness. She was saved by the fact that she had to get ready to open up her secondhand shop, which gave her a way to end the conversation gracefully.

Not long after she went down the hall to the back room, she heard the unfamiliar sound of someone else's footsteps coming down the stairs. "Hi!" she called out from where she was tagging the clothes that had come in the day before. "Come on back."

The footsteps approached, and when she looked up, she was immediately glad that she had already greeted him. This way, Prince Lucas was completely unaware that he had stolen the very breath from her lungs for the third time in twenty-four hours, by the mere fact of his presence.

"Good morning." As he returned her greeting, he crossed the threshold, thereby making the small room smaller. He seemed to be waiting for her to say something. Finally he asked, "Well, what do you think?"

At a loss as to how to respond, Annah took a step

away from him in an attempt to lessen the impact of the whole. She tore her gaze from the mesmerizing depths of his gray eyes, and some of the details started to register. For one thing, his more casual appearance in jeans and a fisherman's knit sweater edged the ruggedness in his looks up a notch, and showed his broad shoulders and tapered hips to splendid advantage. Then she looked at his face, and her mouth dropped.

"You really did it," she said in amazement. His wonderfully thick beard was gone, replaced by a tantalizing expanse of freshly shaven skin. Without realizing what she was doing, she raised her palm and stroked it along the firm, strong jawline that was now exposed. Her thumb traced the masculine hollow under his cheekbone.

Somewhere inside Luke, this sensual assault unleashed a torrent of lava. It flowed through his veins, hot and uncontrolled and so unexpected that it amazed him. It wasn't purely sexual—although there was that, too—and that in and of itself was something new for him. He looked at her with fresh eyes. Her ordinary brown hair suddenly seemed extraordinarily touchable, her medium build fleshed out into enticing, womanly curves, and those lush lips were a lure few men could resist. Raising his eyes, he found himself drawn into the warm depths of hers, as sinfully tempting as the richest chocolate, but with the promise of being far more nourishing to the soul.

Several moments passed before he wondered how much time he had let lapse since she had spoken. He cleared his throat, she withdrew her hand, and the spell ceased, although somehow it didn't seem to be completely broken. "Do you think it's a good enough disguise, Annah?" he asked.

She knew that somehow she would know him any-where, in an instant—she hadn't even noticed that the beard was gone at first. But to answer his question she had to set aside the fact that she herself, for some rea-son, seemed to be super aware of him. "It's good, Your Highness," she answered truthfully.

"Name's Luke. Luke Hansson."

His introduction sounded natural. And the name fit. He looked like a Luke Hansson, rough and rugged and ready to drag some lucky woman off to his marriage bed.

"Do I look like an ordinary man?"

She stared at him a moment, at a loss as to how to answer his question. "Well, you don't look...princely, if that's what you mean." *Ordinary* was what you saw walking down the street every day, not what was stand-ing in front of her. But her personal reaction to him was just that. Personal. "We're going to have to keep you out of that suit you had on yesterday, though."

"My wardrobe of casual clothes is not extensive."

She spread her arms wide. "You've come to the right place. Clothes are my business. My other busi-ness." At the look on his face she had to laugh. "Don't worry, Your Highness. Your being ordinary doesn't have to extend to wearing used clothing. I don't carry men's clothing here, anyway."

He looked around him at the shelves and racks that were fully stocked. "You don't?"

"No. My store does best with what I call high-turnover clothes. Things that don't get worn much be-fore they don't fit anymore, like kids' clothes and ma-ternity clothes. And also, things that people don't want to wear more than a few times, like dressy dresses," she explained. "I don't have any demand for men's clothes. But I do have connections." She went to her desk and dug out a catalog. "Here," she said, handing it to him. "While I'm working, you can go shopping. I have a friend who works for them. She'll make sure anything you want gets here yesterday."

"Me? Go *shopping?*" He said it the way other people might say *bungee jumping*.

"By phone. It's simple. Just find the things you like, then call up and order them. What size are you?"

"Size?"

He was utterly clueless. Obviously princes didn't buy their clothing off the rack. "Never mind," she said. "We'll do it together. It'll be fun."

"Fun?"

This time he was teasing, and she knew it. "It's always fun, spending someone else's money," she joked back.

"That reminds me. We haven't discussed the matter of compensation."

She laughed. "Just give me matchmakers' union wages."

"I mean for my staying here."

"Oh, please." She waved her hand in dismissal. "The room's there. It's unoccupied."

"But I'll need to use your phone. I can't stop working altogether."

"Fine. Reimburse me for your calls."

"What about meals?"

"I have to eat, anyway. It's no more trouble to cook for two."

"But it's more food," he argued.

She shrugged. "So, we'll take turns doing the shopping." At the look on his face she quickly added, "Don't worry. I'll show you how, first. And then you'll want to do it all the time. The local grocery store is a great place to meet women. And that's why you're here, not to hole up in my house and run your country long-distance.''

He gave her a smile, the first that his beard hadn't concealed. She got an instant temperature boost. "You're tough, lady."

"You bet. I'm not letting up until you find what you're looking for," she said briskly. "The search is officially on. First let's take your measurements so we can get started on the new wardrobe you're going to need."

"You're the boss."

"Don't you forget it," she quipped, digging her tape measure out of a drawer. But as she approached him, it became increasingly apparent that this was a bad idea. "Oh-kay," she said, drawing out the word to stall for time. "We'll start with your...height." The idea had been inspired. She just had to look at him to see that he was a perfect six inches taller than she was. "Six feet?"

"Yes."

She wrote it in the margin of the catalog, then turned back to him. "Next, your—" she hesitated, trying to think of a safe area of the body. "Your sleeve," she said.

He stood obediently while she took the measurement and wrote it down. She licked her lips, which had gone dry. "Now your chest," she said with resolve, and came at him from behind.

"Are you sure you know what you're doing?" he asked.

"Of course I'm sure. I'm a professional." After several attempts to reach around him without touching him, she gave up and walked around the front of him.

He fingered his sweater. "Because when my tailor does this, I'm usually not wearing—"

"Well, this is how we do it in America." She would just subtract an inch from the measurement. "Arms up," she ordered.

She gave it a try, but the sweater was too bulky, after all. "All right, now we'll do it without the sweater."

He stripped it over his head, and Annah immediately felt as if she were wearing it now herself. He was in a sleeveless, ribbed T-shirt that made it very clear why that particular garment was commonly referred to as a muscle shirt. She had never seen such well-defined pectorals, up close and personal. Then again, this was the first time she had taken measurements on someone who didn't have a bustline.

"That's all you have on underneath?" she blurted out.

He shrugged, which made the muscles in his shoulders flex. If he did that again, her core temperature would reach critical levels. As it was, her face must be glowing. Her emergency instincts on full alert, she noticed that the bottle of water she used to spray her plants was within easy reach in case she needed an douse. "Hasn't the concept of layering made it to your homeland yet?" she asked.

Her reaction was too obvious for him to mistake. He felt as randy as a moose. "This is Maine. It is not cold enough for that here," he scoffed.

"Well, not *now,*" she muttered, fanning herself with the catalog. Then she took a deep breath and started.

He tried to stand still as a statue, but it took an effort.

Now it was his reaction that concerned him, and it was of growing concern. As she positioned the measuring tape around his chest, she touched him lightly, almost daintily. But that was enough.

She did his waist next, sliding her forefinger between the tape and his body, which made him suck in his breath in response. "Are you holding your stomach in?" she asked suspiciously.

"No!"

"Exhale," she commanded, and after he did she took the measurement again. Her fingers never moved on the tape.

See? he wanted to say, but didn't. He had just realized what measurement was left to take.

Apparently, she had too. Her cheeks were glowing. "Now," she said, and stopped. She cleared her throat. "Now for your inseam."

He took the tape from her. "I'm holding the top of this thing," he growled.

"I have a better idea," she said. "Take off your pants."

Annah watched as he slowly raised one eyebrow. "I'm beginning to understand why my friends sent me to America to find the ideal woman."

"Real funny, royal-boy," she said, hands on hips. "Just go and get me a pair of your pants, so I can use them to get your inseam measurement."

There was a knock at the back door. "Mail's in!" a cheery voice called out. By then Luke had disappeared down the hallway, pulling on his sweater as he went. With one last, longing look at the plant sprayer, Annah opened up the door.

"Hi, there!" Terri Gaines was the sole postal worker in the town. She was tall, blond and was always trying to lose the ten extra pounds that she didn't realize looked good on her. She was friendly and energetic and everyone loved her. "You locked me out today," she said as she stepped inside.

"Sorry, Terri. I was, um, working on a new project, and I guess I lost track of the time."

"I thought I heard voices," Terri said as she looked around the empty room. Then her eyes rested on Annah. "Annah, your cheeks are as red as a lobster! What's going on?" she asked with casual amusement. "Do you have a man in here or something?"

"Yes, but—"

"You *do?*" Terri's eyes rounded.

Annah tried to downplay it. "That was Luke that you heard," she said. "He just got here yesterday, and he's going to be staying with me for a while."

"You've got a man *living* with you?" Terri laughed good-naturedly. "Go, girl! That'll raise a few eyebrows in this ol' town."

"It's not what you think," Annah protested. "There's nothing…romantic between us. Luke's a friend." She laughed and then continued casually, "In fact, I'd be glad to have someone take him off my hands while he's here. You know what a nuisance bachelors can be. Always underfoot."

Just then Luke entered the room. "See what I mean?" she added. "Here he is now."

"I beg your pardon," Luke said, stopping. "I didn't know you had company."

Terri stared at him for a moment before turning back to Annah. "I see what you mean," she said dryly. "What a terrible nuisance to have a man like him around."

Annah let that go and answered Luke. "This isn't

company,'' she said, taking the pants that he had brought down with him. "This is my mailman.''

"Mail*man?*''

Terri laughed. "Political correctness hasn't quite caught hold around here,'' she said, holding out her hand. "Hi. I'm Terri Gaines.''

He shook her hand and said, without stumbling, "Luke Hansson.''

"Nice to meet you, Luke,'' she said, and just like that they were on a first-name basis.

"And you…Terri,'' he added cautiously. He had no idea what to say next. The thrill of going undercover was fast being replaced by the fear of screwing up. He looked at Annah out of the corner of his eye, hoping she would throw him a lifeline, but she just gave him an encouraging smile. He turned back to Terri. "Are you from Anders Point?'' he asked.

"Sure am. What brings you here, Luke?''

What was he supposed to say? They hadn't gone over this yet. This time Annah must have sensed his rising panic, because she jumped back into the conversation.

"Luke's got a big deadline looming, so he decided to take some time away to get a fresh perspective,'' she said. "He had an interest in this area, and I offered to let him stay with me.''

It was all true. Luke was impressed.

So was Terri. "What sort of work do you do?'' she asked him.

Again, he drew a blank, and Annah stepped in to save him.

"He's in management,'' she said. "A family business. You know, passed down from father to son, that sort of thing.''

One thing was for sure. His matchmaker had nerve. Preparation or no preparation, she was going to pull him through this, whether he wanted to do it or not.

"I wonder if I've heard of it," Terri said.

Annah shrugged noncommittally. "They don't do business around here."

Terri's curiosity was still alive and kicking. "Where do you live, Luke?" she asked.

He couldn't *not* answer such a direct question. "I've done so much traveling in my, uh, work, that I'm at home all over the world," he said truthfully.

"Sounds exciting. Where are you from originally?"

With a vague wave of his hand, he said, "Oh, from out in the middle."

"Another Midwesterner, like Annah," Terri said, misunderstanding, to his relief. "You'd better watch it, or you might fall in love with this place, too."

"He might if he had a chance to see it," Annah put in. "But my shop opens in a few minutes, and it'll be dark when I close up, so I can't play tour guide."

Terri didn't let Annah's blatant hint pass her by. "If you want, Luke, you can come on my mail run with me," she offered.

Alone with her, without Annah to help him out? Luke was definitely not ready for this. He shook his head. "Really, you don't need to feel obligated, just because—"

"What a great idea!" Annah broke in. "There's no better way to see the town. Terri covers every square foot of it."

"I don't feel obligated," Terri added warmly. "In fact, I'd love the company. I'll even buy you lunch at Kelvin's. Their fried chicken is worth the trip to Anders Point."

"See?" Annah said, turning to him. "There's an offer you can't refuse." There was no mistaking the look in her eyes. He was going, if she had to stuff him into Terri's mailbag.

"Great!" Terri said. "Grab your coat, Luke. I'll be right back. I've got another package for Annah, out in the truck."

As soon as the door banged closed, Annah gave him a triumphant grin. "How's that for matchmaking?" she said excitedly. "You've been here less than twenty-four hours and you're going on your first date!"

He felt less inclined to celebrate. "That was a real...surprise," he said.

"What do you think of her?" Annah asked, without giving him time to answer. "Isn't she cute? And nice? And friendly? Luke, how do you like her?"

"I like her fine," he said truthfully. "But I don't like the idea of being alone with her." Even a few minutes had been nerve-racking.

"It's just for the afternoon."

The whole afternoon? He felt his mouth drop open.

"Don't worry," she told him. "You'll do fine. Just be yourself."

"Oh, now *that's* helpful," he said testily, spurred on by a full-blown case of first-date jitters. "Annah, I'm a *prince*. What experience in my life do you suggest I draw upon in order to successfully ride shotgun in a mail truck with a stranger named Terri?"

She crossed her arms and glared at him. "Do you want a princess or not?" she asked.

"You know I do," he said, glaring right back.

"Then listen up, Your Highness. This woman gets the matchmaking gold seal of approval. She meets all your requirements, plus she's interested in you. She asked you out, Luke! Do you want to pass up a chance like this?''

"You could have given me a little more time to prepare."

"Does the phrase *lost opportunity* mean anything to you?" she asked. "How many single women do you think there are in a little town like this, anyway?"

"Is this your idea of a pep talk?"

"I mean it, Luke," she warned. "If you're not careful, you'll need more than a matchmaker. You'll need a miracle worker. Just loosen up and improvise."

He saw his whole kingdom pass before his eyes. "Improvisation has never been my strong suit."

"Hush," Annah said, looking out the window. "She's coming back."

It was inevitable now. He had gotten himself into this, and now he would have to see it through. Squaring his shoulders, he said, "Any last words of advice that will keep me from blowing my cover?"

"Yes. Eat the fried chicken with your fingers, Your Highness."

Chapter Four

It took Luke a moment or two to orient himself when he awoke the next morning. He wasn't in his palatial bedroom suite in the Constellation Isles, stretched out in the luxuriant, satin-clad bed that dwarfed even him—he could lie in the middle of it and not be able to reach any of the edges.

No, he was half a world away, tucked into a large closet under the eaves that Annah referred to, in all seriousness, as her spare bedroom. The bed, swathed in soft flannel sheets and plump with a down comforter, embraced him like a cozy little nest. A second pillow lay empty next to his, which made him wonder. Did some married couples really share a bed this small? His parents hadn't even shared a room.

He imagined a wife lying on the bed next to him, soft and warm. There would be no way to avoid touching each other. A good lovemaking bed. A good *baby*-making bed.

The unfamiliar sounds of rattling dishes and of talk

and laughter drifted into his room, a welcome distraction from the turn his thoughts had taken. It was barely light outside, but Annah's day was apparently in full swing, despite the fact that she hadn't been home yet when he'd gone to sleep the night before. He'd come home from his tour of the town with Terri to an empty house. In the last room he checked—the kitchen—he'd found a brief note from Annah on the table, a sandwich in the refrigerator and a huge slice of melt-in-yourmouth chocolate cake on the counter. He would have liked to confer with his matchmaker after his first date, but she was one busy lady. No wonder she didn't want kids in her life.

The image of the wife lying next to him popped into his mind again, and her hair wasn't blond like Terri's, it was brown like...no, not even in a mirage could he let his wife be Annah. Annah was all wrong for him—even he could see that. He turned onto his stomach and clamped both pillows over his head, which shut out the sights of her house and the sound of her customers and the beckoning smell of her coffee. But it didn't shut out the feel of the bed shifting under a new weight next to him, or the feel of hands walking up the back of him, from his legs to his shoulders. He peered through a crack in the pillows and saw an eye staring back at him. But it wasn't brown. And it wasn't human.

He sat up quickly, flinging the pillows aside, ready to confront the green-eyed beast. A large gray tigerstriped cat perched on the bed beside him. Unconcerned by his sudden motion, it walked gingerly over the comforter and climbed onto his legs again, settling into a seat this time. "Rauw," it said, looking up at him expectantly.

Luke stared back. No cat had ever sat on him before. "Get...off...me!" he said, in a voice that made brigadier generals tremble.

"Rauw," the cat repeated, without blinking an eye or budging an inch.

"That's it," Luke said. He rolled the cat off his legs and got out of bed before it could settle on him again. He'd have thought Annah would have told him she had a cat—unless she'd been too busy for that, too. Still, it seemed strange that he hadn't seen it before, or any food dishes, either. The cat stared at him from the middle of the disheveled bedcovers, looking plainly miffed at having been shunted aside. But after Luke finished dressing, it launched itself off the bed and passed him on the stairs. Luke followed it into the kitchen and found it sitting at the door to the backyard.

"Rauw," it said insistently, louder than before. As if on command Luke opened the door, and after giving him a look that oozed condescension the cat strolled nonchalantly out and disappeared around the corner of the house.

Glad that was taken care of, Luke decided to stop ignoring the wonderful aromas from down the hall. He followed his nose into the coffee shop. Unlike the first time he had seen it, it was full of light and bustling with people. Apparently the proprietor did quite a business here.

She didn't notice him at first, as he stood there in the inner doorway. And no wonder. She was doing at least six things, all at the same time, and balancing a trayful of dirty dishes in the meantime. How did she manage it? He watched, intrigued. He didn't move or make a sound, but somehow Annah knew he was there. She stopped in the middle of carrying her tray over to the counter and looked right at him. Her eyes always went wide and soft when she first looked at him. He liked that. And then her lips spread into that familiar, wise smile.

"Hi, Luke," she greeted him, setting down the tray. "Don't just stand there. There's an empty stool at the counter that's got your name on it. Right between Wilfred and Eldridge."

It was, in fact, the only empty seat in the place. He settled into it, nodding politely at the two older men who were seated at either side. They nodded back, then turned their attention to the pastries in front of them. Annah brought him a mug of coffee—black and strong, which she somehow knew was his preference—then hurried off to set places at a recently vacated table for some new arrivals. Luke drank his coffee and silently took in his surroundings. There was a good deal of talk among the patrons, and snatches of conversation floated his way amid the clinking of silverware and the scrape of wooden chair legs on the linoleum.

"My boy Tom's coming home for the Firehouse Dance, Annah," an older woman at the table behind him said. "If you're free, he'd be pleased to escort you."

"Thanks, Edna, but I'm—"

"In charge of the refreshments for the dance," chimed in a number of voices from the neighboring tables in unison with Annah's reply.

"Well, I am!" she said, laughing. "I didn't hear anyone else volunteering to do it at the planning meeting."

"Now, dear," another gray-haired woman said, in a clucking, mother-hen kind of voice. "We all know you're the best person for the job. It's just that we still want you to have fun at the dance.''

"I'm planning to," Annah assured her as she breezed back behind the counter.

The woman went on. "And my Edward is just the one to—"

"Forget it," Edna snapped at her. "If she didn't want my Tom, she won't want your Edward.''

"It's nothing personal—" Annah began.

"She should have *someone* for a date," a third voice offered.

"Why?" Annah asked with a saucy grin. "Ladies, a girl who doesn't have a date can dance with all the boys."

That statement got her out of the hot seat by starting a heated discussion among her customers. Luke found himself grinning, too.

"What's the Firehouse Dance?" he asked her, but she was already off taking an order to a table across the room.

"Big to-do in town," answered Eldridge, the old man on his left, who had been silent until now.

"Takes place in the old firehouse," chimed in Wilfred, the one on his right.

"That's why the name," added Eldridge.

"Charity thing."

"Ayup."

Luke had already found out that last sound passed for the affirmative around here. "When is it?" he asked.

"Month or so," said Eldridge.

"Smack between Thanksgiving and Christmas," said Wilfred.

"Long enough so those biddies will drive our Annah crazy."

Wilfred gave a snort of contempt. "Trying to fix her up with their sons and nephews and grandsons."

"Ayup," Eldridge replied. "Getting so's a man can't set down to drain a cup of joe without having to abide with all that cackling."

"Ayup."

Then Annah walked over with refills for the three of them. His two companions addressed her as if Luke was mute.

"This the fellow you're living in sin with?" Wilfred asked, jerking a thumb at Luke.

Luke gripped the edge of the counter and started to rise. Annah put a hand on his and silently shook her head. He sat slowly back down.

"That's right, Wilfred," Annah replied.

Six eyebrows shot up. "That is, if you consider it a sin to offer a spare room to a friend," she added.

"Be your friend staying long?" asked Eldridge.

"Back off, Eldridge," snapped Wilfred.

"Just want to know if he's staying till the Firehouse Dance. Nice feller. He could take Annah, and then those biddies would stop cackling."

"Wouldn't, neither. They'd start setting a wedding date."

Eldridge thought about that for a minute, taking several long slurps of coffee. Luke watched him, waiting. "Ayup," he finally said. And that was the end of that.

Luke looked up at Annah to see her reaction to all this, but she was gone again, wiping off the other end of the counter. The crowd was starting to thin. Wilfred and Eldridge set down their empty cups and put some money on the counter, then left him sitting between two empty stools.

Annah came over to clear away their dishes. "Heard it went great yesterday afternoon," she said in a low voice.

"How did you—"

"Terri was in before. She was disappointed not to see you."

"I guess I did all right, then."

Annah laughed. "Yeah. You were passable," she said, rolling her eyes. "Terri *always* gets out of bed at six on her only day off just for a cup of my coffee." She turned serious then. "But, tell me. How did you like her?"

"She was very nice. Down-to-earth. The afternoon went by quickly."

"I guess that means you enjoyed it."

"I guess I did," he said cautiously. "But I'm not saying I want to marry her."

"No one said you had to say that now. Go out with her again. Time will tell."

He frowned at the bottom of his coffee cup while she went to wait on some new arrivals. He just hoped time didn't take too long to tell, or he'd be an ordinary guy permanently.

Annah went back behind the counter to fill the new order. He watched her pour coffee and fill a tray with muffins and Danish. She saw him looking, and sent him a smile. "Sorry I couldn't make a real dinner for you last night," she said. "All I had time for was leftovers."

He didn't want her worrying about waiting on him. She was busy enough, and he preferred she save any extra energy for matchmaking. "Leftovers are my fa-

vorite meal,'' he said, with all the seriousness he could
muster.

''As *if*,'' she said, propping one hand on her hip and
grinning.

As if he had ever had them before. She might as
well have come out and said it. ''Really, Annah. The
sandwich was great. What kind was it, anyway?''

She stared at him. ''Haven't you ever had a cold
meat loaf sandwich before?''

He shook his head. ''Culturally deprived.''

''I guess so,'' she said, laughing. He liked the way
she enjoyed his humor. People were afraid to laugh at
a prince, so being able to have conversations like this
was a nice byproduct of his disguise.

''Will you make it again sometime?''

''Sure. I'll even let you try it hot,'' she said, a twinkle in her eye.

He wondered where she had been the night before,
but didn't feel it was his place to ask. Then something
occurred to him. ''Annah,'' he began cautiously. ''Is
my living in your house in any way...inconvenient for
you?''

''What do you mean?''

I mean, were you out on a date last night? he
thought. He looked around, but no one seemed to be
paying any attention to them. ''Socially,'' he said at
last. ''Socially inconvenient.''

She blushed, so he knew that she understood what
he meant. ''No,'' she said, not looking quite at him.
''It isn't.''

''Because if you want to go out with that Tom or
Edward, I can—''

''No, really,'' she said. ''I'm too busy to date much.
And anyway, I hate getting fixed up.''

"I know the feeling," he said quietly.

"Touché." She met his eyes, and gave him an encouraging smile. "I know you don't love the process, but it's the product that counts, right?"

"Ayup."

She laughed. "Sounds like you're getting acclimated."

"Ayup."

"I do want to hear about your date with Terri. I'm sorry I wasn't in last night, but Mrs. Cartelli down the street got the unexpected news that her sister in Connecticut passed away, so I went and sat with her awhile."

"Sat with her?"

"Yes. She and her sister were very close. Her daughter came this morning to take her to Connecticut, but I just couldn't stand the thought of her grieving all alone last night."

He knew how that felt. No one had "sat with" him after his father had died unexpectedly the year before. Not that he had expected anyone to. He didn't have any other family; it was not the place of his staff; and it probably wouldn't have occurred to his friends Erik and Whit—just as it wouldn't have occurred to him. But it did to Annah. If he had known her then, she would have sat with him, offering comfort as naturally as she was offering him her house, her time, her friendship now.

A sudden thought occurred to him. "Do we have a cat?" he asked her.

She smiled. "Temporarily," she said. "Just until Mrs. Cartelli comes home again. Did Purrkins introduce himself?"

"Not by name." *Purrkins?* Just the kind of silly

name a cat would have. A name Luke would never say out loud, he vowed to himself. "In fact he introduced himself rather rudely, by jumping on the bed."

"He did?" Annah sounded surprised. "He must really like you, Luke. He's normally very shy around strangers."

"Lucky me."

"Where is he now? I left him upstairs because I couldn't bring him in here with me. Health regulations."

Luke shrugged. "He's outside somewhere."

"Outside? Luke, you let him *out?*"

"Of course I did. The cat led me to the door and practically ordered me to open it."

"Oh, no." Annah sounded worried. "Luke, didn't you see my note? I left strict orders not to let him out. Purrkins is a house cat."

Luke was not used to anyone leaving him notes, especially with orders in them. "Well, if he's a house cat, I guess he went back to his house," he said with a shrug.

She planted her hands on her hips. "Luke, you have to go and get him!"

"Me? Why me?"

"You let him out," she argued from behind the counter. "Besides, I'm working. Unless you want to take over here for me."

She had him there. He could no more run the coffee shop than he could fly around the room, and they both knew it. He frowned at her. "I'm sure it can wait until you close up."

She glanced at the clock. Then she looked out of the side window, down the street, lost in thought. "The timing should be perfect," she mumbled to herself.

"What timing?"

She looked at him. "I mean, the timing is…awful, for him to wait until I close up," she said, her brows drawn together with worry. "Luke, he's declawed. He can't defend himself out there. Any second something could happen to him, and then how will I explain to poor Mrs. Cartelli?"

Luke knew when he was beat. He got to his feet, throwing his napkin onto the counter. "All right," he muttered. "I'll go rescue the poor defenseless beast."

After his tour of the town yesterday, Luke needed only the briefest of directions from Annah before he set out. Anders Point was a town to feel at home in, centered on an open area of grass and trees called the common. The houses in town were more than a century old or fast approaching it, and they sat companionably close, as if to brave the elements together, on small but well-kept plots of land. Things spread out a little on the castle road—the house on the end belonged to Whit's wife, Drew—but overall the town was cheerfully compact. Of course, its growth would naturally be limited by its closest neighbor, the ocean, which surrounded the finger of land on which the town was situated. The castle sat at the end, high on a bluff, looking out across the waters of the Atlantic to the island home of its owners, Isle Anders. The sea, of course, had always been the dominant force in the life of the town. Even now, employment depended on it, fishing boats sharing the waters with those whose primary catch was tourists. Those were not too numerous, because of the town's remote location, he had been told. And now, in November, only residents populated the town. He was the only outsider who walked among them.

Mrs. Cartelli's house was just as Annah had described it. And sure enough, curled up on the front doorstep was the cat that had possessed the audacity to sit on him.

"Hello again, beast," he said.

The cat ignored him, pretending to be wholly absorbed in the process of wetting his paw and running it over his whiskers. Luke watched him do it about seventeen times while he tried to figure out how to get him from here to Annah's house. Annah had tried to give him a leash, but he figured he might just as well dress up as a clown and walk down the street on his hands as walk a cat down the street on a leash. A box would work, but he didn't see any lying around Mrs. Cartelli's yard. He wondered what would happen if he tried to pick the cat up, then quickly decided he really didn't care to find out. Maybe the damn cat would just follow him, although he doubted it.

"Come on, beast," he said. "Let's go back to Annah's."

The cat made a show of yawning unconcernedly and closing his eyes.

"His name's not Beast," said a voice at Luke's elbow. "It's Purrkins. Are you trying to kidnap him?"

Luke started, then looked down. A little girl of about six stood next to him. She was wearing a blue wool coat and had a big pink satin bow in her dark hair.

"You can't *kid*nap a cat. You have to *kit*-nap him," came a voice at his other elbow. It was another little girl, just like the first one except that her bow was yellow. "And anyway," she said decidedly. "He's not a bad stranger. Mommy said he's the man who's staying with Annah. She said we could talk to him.''

"I'm Luke," he said, hunkering down so he was at eye level with them.

"I'm Jenny," said the one with the pink bow.

"I'm Janine."

"Pleased to meet you, Jenny and Janine," he said, doing the best bow he could manage from a squat.

"Why are you here?" Janine asked bluntly.

"Well, Annah wants me to get Purr—this cat—back to her house. She's watching him for Mrs. Cartelli.''

"I bet he let him out," Janine said to Jenny, who nodded.

The twins were on to him. And they were cute as the dickens. "I did," Luke confessed soberly. "I didn't know he was a house cat. And now Annah's pretty sore at me.''

Both girls looked at him sympathetically. "Well, the good part is he's not lost. All you have to do it take him back," Jenny said.

Janine was looking at him intently. "You don't know how to get him there, do you?" she asked him at last.

"Well, no," he admitted.

"Didn't you ever have a cat, mister?"

"No. My mother didn't allow pets in the pal—I mean, in the house.''

This aroused some sympathy for his cause. "Oh, you poor thing!" Jenny said. "Our mommy does. She's really nice. We have a cat and a dog and a rabbit and a bird.''

Janine sighed. "The only thing we don't have is a daddy. Ours died when we were babies.''

"Oh. I'm sorry," Luke said. Poor kids.

He caught a secret look between them before Jenny said, "It would be nice to have a daddy."

"Yes. And Mommy needs one, too," Janine put in. "Poor Mommy has no one to sit with her at our piano recital on Thursday."

"Look. Here comes Mommy now."

Luke saw a dark-haired woman leaving the house two doors down.

"Isn't she pretty?" Janine asked him.

"Very," Luke observed. She had the girls' wavy black hair, and enough curves to make any man take a second look.

"Okay, here's the deal," whispered Janine quickly. "We'll take Purrkins to Annah's house for you on our way to church. But you have to do something for us."

Five minutes later he walked back into the coffee shop, a little dazedly. Annah was grinning at him from behind the counter, where she was polishing up glasses. The place was nearly empty. "I see you got some reinforcements to help you round up the ferocious beast," she said.

He slid back onto his seat. "Got a problem, call in someone with the expertise to help you."

She laughed. "That's why you came to me, isn't it?"

"Joke if you want, but those two could put you right out of the matchmaking business."

"Let me guess—you're taking Marilyn to the twins' piano recital on Thursday?"

He stared at her. "How did you know?"

She bobbed her eyebrows playfully. "Why else would I have sent you their way?"

So that was what she had meant by timing. She knew

they'd be walking by at that time, on their way to church. "I take it, then, that Marilyn is preapproved?"

"Absolutely. She was widowed five years ago, so she's ready to move on." Then something occurred to her. She put her elbows on the counter and leaned in toward him. "It *is* okay that she's been married before, isn't it?"

She was so close. If he leaned toward her a fraction, he would find out how those lush lips of hers tasted. "Yes," he answered, trying to focus on the conversation. "Of course, her children wouldn't be in line for the throne, but as long as she is willing to have more—"

"I have reason to believe she is," Annah murmured.

"Then there's nothing wrong with her being a widow, as far as my country is concerned." Something made him want to test the waters. After a split second's pause he added, "My marrying a divorcée would be fine, too. That is, as long as she would be willing to have my babies."

Annah stood up abruptly. "I can't think of anyone like that here in town," she said. "But I'm glad you've got something set up with Marilyn. I think you'll like her." Then the front door opened, and she went around the counter—too quickly, Luke thought—to greet her customer.

A few minutes later she came over to him with the new arrival in tow. "There's someone I want you to meet," Annah was saying to the woman. "This is my friend Luke, who's staying with me for a while."

Luke stood up. "This is Shannon Rafferty," she told him. "Shannon's a friend of mine."

Shannon had a lovely air of self-possession, an elegant carriage, shoulder-length auburn hair and eyes the color of the maple syrup on the counter. Luke took the hand she held out. "How do you do?" she greeted him politely.

"Very well, thank you," he replied as he shook the hand she held out. He would have bet the palace that this woman had never said "Ayup" in her life.

Annah, back behind the counter, set a cup of espresso at the place next to Luke's. "Shannon just got off the night shift at the hospital, so she's here for a little eye-opener before church," she explained to him. He sat back down after Shannon took her seat, noticing that the shop was now empty except for the three of them.

"Is that where everyone went?" he asked.

"Just about everyone," Annah told him. "Don't worry. We'll still be able to make the service on time."

He turned to Shannon while Annah stacked dirty dishes in the dishwasher. "What sort of work do you do at the hospital?" he asked, pleased at the way he had learned that was a good way to start a conversation when you were an ordinary guy.

"I'm a nurse," she told him.

"An OB nurse," Annah added, giving him a meaningful look. At his slight shrug, she explained, "Obstetrics," and then he got it. Babies. His matchmaker was telling him that the woman sitting on the stool next to him liked babies. Annah was also giving him not-so-subtle eye signals to continue the conversation. So he knew Shannon had the gold seal of approval, too.

"Any born last night?" he asked her.

"Six at the hospital. Two were mine."

"Ah," Annah sighed, leaning on the counter. "Boys or girls?"

"Beautiful little girls," Shannon told her.

Luke was watching Annah's reaction with interest, wondering if her interest in the babies was just a show to keep him talking with the nurse. She noticed his eyes on her, and busied herself with cleaning up again.

Feeling the need to pick up the conversational ball, Luke turned back to Shannon. "Have you lived here at the Point all your life?" he asked.

"Except for college."

"Where was that?"

"In Boston."

"And one semester overseas, as an exchange student," Annah added.

No wonder she seemed cosmopolitan. As soon as that thought crossed his mind, he wanted to laugh. It was not a word he would have used to describe an Anders Point woman a few days ago. Then, Shannon would have been just a quiet, hometown girl. Which just showed how his point of orientation had shifted already.

Annah filled the silence. "Speaking of overseas, they're playing a great foreign film at the Bijou tonight. That's the old movie theater here in town," she explained to Luke. "Would you be interested in going, Shannon?"

"Sure. I'm off tonight," Shannon said. Then she seemed to think better of it and added, "But I don't want to intrude on your plans. I mean, if the two of you..."

"Nonsense," Annah told her. "Luke and I are just friends. Anyway, I can't go myself, so it will just be the two of you. You'll be doing me a favor by keeping Luke company."

"Well, if you put it that way," Shannon said. "I

know I owe you several favors, Annah. See you in church.''

"Brava," Luke said after Shannon had left. "That was a neat little matchmaking trick you just pulled there.''

Annah grinned. "*I* thought so," she said. "So what do you think of her?''

"I'm thinking I'm not sure I can keep a conversation going with this one. Terri took care of that part yesterday.''

"Yes, Shannon is quiet until you get to know her, but remember, still waters run deep. That's why I thought a movie would be good for a first date. You'll just have to walk there and back, really. And sit next to her in the dark for two hours.'' She paused, then added, "Use some body language. I hear it's a steamy flick.''

She gave him a naughty grin, and he thought then that he would much rather be sitting next to her tonight than with a woman who had been tricked into going out with him. With Annah, he felt like he could be himself....

Whoever that was.

They arrived at church just before the service started, and Annah chose a pew where an attractive honey blonde sat next to an older woman. To his surprise, when the children were dismissed for church school, Annah got up and left, too, leaving him sitting next to the blonde.

It took him a while after the service ended to locate Annah in the crowd.

"Hi!" she said as he walked up to her. She stepped

aside with him so they could talk in private. "How was the service?"

"Fine," he said. "Why weren't you there to find out for yourself?"

"I'm teaching this trimester, so I only get to stay for the first part."

"You teach church school?" he asked, surprised.

She smiled. "Ayup. Sixth grade."

"Why?" he asked. "Won't anyone else volunteer to do that, either?" Like taking care of the refreshments for the dance. Like sitting with Mrs. Cartelli. Like helping him find a wife. Annah was a person you could count on. He would bet that Shannon wasn't the only person in town who owed Annah a favor or two.

"Well, it's not most people's most popular age group," she admitted laughingly. "But I do it because I happen to enjoy it. The kids in my class are great."

Babies weren't her thing, but preadolescent kids were? He couldn't figure that one out, so he filed it away for the future. "Listen, Annah, would you mind walking home alone?"

Her eyes went wide. "Did you get another date?"

"Actually, I was recruited to move tables and chairs for a Ladies' Mission Society meeting this afternoon." He looked at her narrowly. "Was this your doing, too?"

Annah shook her head, laughing. "Not what I had in mind when I sat you with Carol Carson and her mother. But this is great! It just goes to show how much you look like a regular guy. Do you think they would have asked a prince to do this?"

He hadn't thought of it quite that way.

"I'll bet you'll have another date before you're finished. Go show off those muscles," she said, squeezing his biceps. He flexed it involuntarily at her touch, and she dropped her hand abruptly. "I, um, I've got to get going."

She started to turn away, but he grabbed her arm. "Not so fast. You've been so busy, we still haven't really had a chance to talk. About this whole...strategy, I mean."

"Luke, in case you haven't noticed, things are moving along nicely on their own."

"Things are moving *quickly.*"

"So's your deadline," she pointed out archly.

But he was persistent. "Annah, I want to talk to you," he said in the commanding tone of a prince. "When can we do that?"

"How about this afternoon? My secondhand shop is closed on Sundays, and I'll be free right after—" She hesitated for a moment, her eyes fixed on something behind him.

"Do you have something else to do?"

"Not anymore," she murmured.

"Excuse me?"

She focused on him again. "Not a thing," she said. "I'll see you anytime this afternoon...anytime you don't have a date, that is."

"But I don't have a date this afternoon. The movie with Shannon isn't until this evening."

"Well, you never know what could come up. Don't pass up a date just to talk to me," she said, wiggling her fingers in goodbye as she left him.

Luke shook his head, watching her cross the room toward the door. He'd already had a date with one woman, and two more to come. But the woman who intrigued him the most wasn't one of his dates. She was the one arranging them.

Chapter Five

Luke got home about half an hour after Annah did, looking a bit dazed.

She knew the look by now. "Got yourself another date, Your Highness?" she asked, grinning.

He shrugged as he passed her. "Carol plays on a coed volleyball team. They were a player short this afternoon, so I'm filling in," he said. "If you call that a date."

"I do!" she called after him up the stairs, which he had taken two at a time. "And I'm glad you didn't worry about standing me up."

"I knew you wouldn't want me to pass up a chance for a *date*." She could hear drawers opening and closing upstairs.

"You're really getting the hang of this, Luke," she said, thoroughly enjoying herself. "I don't think we need to talk. In fact, I don't think you even need me at all."

He poked his head around his bedroom door. His

shoulders and chest were bare. Annah felt a full-body flush coming on.

"I beg to differ. I have a pretty good idea which player they're short, Annah," he said, giving her a direct look.

She was impressed. He must have seen her canceling with Carol on her way out of church. Whoever married him would have to be on her toes, to stay one step ahead of him.

Just then she heard him bark out a short word that had to be a swear in his native language.

"*Rauw!*" came an indignant answer, and Purrkins flew down the stairs, fur ruffled, grumbling to himself.

Annah laughed, and Luke heard her. "It's not funny!" he called down.

"I told you, he likes you!"

"Well, I don't like *him*. I especially don't like him in my sheets," Luke said as he clambered down the stairs wearing sweats. His mahogany hair was all tousled, and she could see his pulse beating on the side on his neck. Elemental man. She wondered how he'd look playing volleyball, his muscles flexing under glistening skin, and—

"And if I find him there again—" he warned.

"If you made your bed, Your Highness..." Annah began sweetly, reminding herself that elemental men had their faults. Especially if they were princes in disguise.

"Until you have time to give me a lesson, I'll close the door," he said gruffly. "That ought to keep him away from where he has no business being."

"Rauw," said Purrkins, who came over to sit on the floor at Luke's feet. Willing to forget the indignity he had suffered at being turned out of the nest of his chosen one, the cat looked up at Luke longingly, as if he wanted to leap into his arms.

Annah couldn't help laughing again.

Luke glared at her. "Just keep that beast away from me," he warned. "And be ready to talk when I get back."

"Yes, Your Highness," she said in mock seriousness, giving him a deep curtsy. "Your wish is my command."

He gave her an inscrutable look from under his brows. "Careful, or I might take you up on that," he murmured as he left.

Annah was in the kitchen when Luke came downstairs, freshly showered after his volleyball game. "What's for dinner?" he asked, standing behind her.

"Yankee pot roast. Did you ever have it before?"

She lifted the lid to show him, and he inhaled deeply. "No, but I love it," he said with a sigh.

"Methinks His Highness is acquainted with the high art of flattery," she said drolly.

"Methinks the cook has forgotten that His Highness is an ordinary man with an ordinary man's appetites."

They looked at each other and then away, both suddenly aware of his unintended double entendre. If he had other appetites, so did she. One in particular that she had neglected for a long time was making its presence known more insistently the more she was around Luke.

What did she expect? she asked herself. The last time she had shared a house with a man, she had been married. Closeness bred familiarity.

But it wasn't just that. She could probably share a house with most men and not feel the slightest twinge of desire. It had to do with this particular man. Whenever he was so much as in the same room with her, she got all fidgety and distracted. She watched him all the time when he wasn't looking. Physically she found him attractive—in the literal sense. She was actually drawn to him, to the point where she had to consciously stop herself from drifting closer to him, from raising her hand to touch him. She didn't remember ever feeling that way about her ex-husband. Luke seemed to fill her little house up.

But her house was big enough for both of them, she lectured herself sternly. And she was old enough to be able to handle being a little hot and bothered while she helped the man out. Still, it was with some relief that she noticed that he had a bundle in his hand, which gave her an opening for ordinary conversation.

"What's that?"

"It's my dirty clothes. We never really discussed the laundry arrangements."

Annah grinned. "Alas, the laundress has the day off."

His Highness was not amused. "I'm running out of clean things to wear. Do you think I'll attract any princesses wearing these?"

"You have a point there," she said, adding, "I should send you to the laundromat in town."

He looked at her skeptically.

"It's a great place to meet single women," she told him. "But since they're closed on Sundays, I guess you'll have to do your laundry here."

"*I* will?"

"Sure. Why not?"

"Because I'll be too busy whipping up a chocolate mousse for dessert," he said dryly.

She laughed and said, "I'm serious. We're talking washing *machine* here. Ordinary men love to operate machinery, Luke."

"You're really reaching, Annah. If you want me to drive a fast sports car, I'm your man. Power tools also hold a definite appeal. But real men don't do washers."

"Sure they do, Luke! I'm not saying they like it, but they do it, and so can you. And then when you go to the laundromat you'll have the general idea of what's going on. Think of it as an ordinary guy lesson." At the rate he was going, he wouldn't need many more of those. He was doing really well with his new role—so well that she was sure no one in town had a hint as to his true identity. Underneath the fancy title, he was a real man.

And he did pretty well on laundry detail, considering he had never even operated a hamper in his palace life. During the wash cycle, Annah helped him pick out some clothes from the catalog and placed the order with her friend.

"Shouldn't we order some more?" he asked after they had sat down to dinner. "That's only enough for a week."

"Good try, but you're not ordering a month's supply of clothes just to get out of doing laundry," she told him. "Besides, people might get suspicious if you're always wearing something new."

"Bah. They won't notice."

"Shows what you know," she retorted. "Women notice these things. Especially when a man wears clothes as well as you do."

He looked up from his plate. "Was that meant as a compliment?" he asked softly.

She met his eyes, and her senses scattered. *Yes. No.*

Oh, God, she didn't know. She looked away. "It's an observation," she said lightly. "We matchmakers are good at that."

After a moment he said, "Not only that, Annah."

"What do you mean?"

"I mean there must be some reason why I'm getting dates with single women at the speed of light."

"It's great, isn't it?" she said. "But I can't take the credit for it."

"No? Then how do you explain it? Believe me, I wasn't having any kind of luck until now."

"That's not surprising, given how you were going about it."

"What do you mean?"

She studied the end of her fork, trying to think of a way to put it into words for him. "What you were doing before was like going fishing on dry land," she finally said. "No matter how hard you tried, you just couldn't have caught what you were fishing for. And then..." She paused.

"Go on," he said with interest, leaning forward.

"Well, then you came here. That was like getting your boat in the water. You became an ordinary man. That's like using the right kind of bait. Naturally the fish are biting now."

"Biting?" he said with a laugh. "Annah, I never even had a chance to get my line wet. The fish just started leaping into the boat."

She gave him that knowing grin. "Do you have a problem with that? If I recall, this is a pretty close approximation of what you wanted."

"I'm not complaining, mind you. It's just that the boat's getting a little full."

She pointed her fork at him. "Don't even think

about throwing any back in yet, Your Highness. You've got to give it time!'' She added, ''There's only one more fish left, anyway, and I think she'll be swimming your way tomorrow.''

''There you go, tossing in another one.''

''Am not! In case you haven't noticed, I haven't made one legitimate fix-up yet. They haven't needed much of a prod to make the leap.'' She thought about it. ''Well, maybe Shannon. But she would have taken a while if I hadn't suggested the movie.''

''That was the most blatant one, I'll grant you that. But, Annah, you were behind every one of these dates and you know it.''

''I just played some hunches, and it paid off.''

''Stop trying to wriggle out of this, and just accept my thanks. You're doing a great job.''

There was a knock at the kitchen door. It was Shannon. Within minutes she and Luke were on their way to the movie, leaving Annah to wish that she wasn't such a good matchmaker after all.

After she closed up the coffee shop the next morning, Annah took Luke to the grocery store. It was nice having her to himself, he thought as they drove there. He had spent the morning at the counter again, wedged between Eldridge and Wilfred, who were as guilty as the ladies they accused of trying to get Annah a date for the Firehouse Dance. She continued to put off all fix-up attempts with patience and good humor.

''I've made a decision,'' he said out loud.

She whipped her head around to look at him. ''You know who you want to marry already?'' she asked. She sounded surprised—and a little dismayed, it seemed to him.

"No, no," he told her. Far from it. "But I have decided that I am going to make my choice by the Firehouse Dance. Getting engaged that night will still leave me with a few weeks before my marriage deadline."

"Good idea. You do have to fit a wedding in there somewhere." She glanced over at him. "How did your date with Shannon go?"

"You were right about the movie. She's very quiet. I'm not sure she even likes me."

"Shannon's not the flirty type."

"Are you sure she fits my requirement?"

"Positive. I know she's seriously considering adopting as a single mother. Luke, she wants a baby in the worst way, poor thing."

Luke looked at her eyes, moistened at the corners in sympathy. Annah actually felt sorry for a woman who wanted to be a mother! He said nothing, because he couldn't think of anything to say that didn't sound judgmental, which he had no right to be.

Before long Annah turned a corner and announced, "Here we are at McCreedy's."

It was no supermarket, but a little, family-run grocery store with wooden shelves crammed to overflowing. Luke looked around, bewildered, at the maze of narrow aisles and unfamiliar displays, while Annah pulled a wire cart out of the queue and pushed it over to him. One wheel wasn't touching the ground, and it rattled noisily. "Here," she said. "You'll need one of these, because there are quite a few items on the list."

"*I'll* need—"

"Here's the list and the car keys."

"Car keys?"

"Well, sure. You'll need the car, to bring all these

groceries home," she said reasonably. "I don't mind walking. I'll be home in a few minutes."

"You're *leaving*?"

"Of course. I have to open up the secondhand shop. You know that, Luke."

He looked down at the list that hung limply in his hand. "You want me to get all this?"

"Yes, and just have them put it on my tab. We'll reconcile it at the end of the month." She glanced at her watch. "I've got to go."

"But I never did this before! I don't know how to shop for groceries."

She winked at him. "You will," she promised.

The secondhand shop was empty when he pulled in the driveway, so Annah went to help him unload the car. "How did it go?" she asked, picking up a bag.

"I was like a bull in a china shop," he growled. "Why didn't you tell me the cart pulled to the right?"

"Uh, oh. Did you hit that toilet paper display?"

"The damn things rolled all over the store! If all those ladies hadn't helped me, I'd still be there trying to round them all up."

"See! I knew your masculine vulnerability would get you through. No woman can resist a helpless man."

"For your information, these women all had little kids in their carts and wedding bands on their fingers."

"Wow. You really know how to read the signs. You must be a seasoned wife hunter," she said, unable to repress a smile. "How did you do grocery shopping? Find everything on the list?"

"Cute, Annah," he said, setting the last bag down on the kitchen floor. "Nice touch, giving me a list with one item that doesn't exist on it."

"Are you accusing me of—"

"Matchmaking? Yes. How did you know that Joyce would come by when I was cruising the cookie aisle?"

"Because that's when her nursery school lets out, and she always goes right out to buy snacks for the next day," Annah said smugly. "So when's your date?"

"It's not a date. I'm going to fix a shelf for her in the reading nook tomorrow morning."

"Date."

"Annah, the kids will be there!"

"Good. You'll get to see her in action. Joyce is great. Mommy material at its finest. Isn't that the whole point?"

"Well, when you put it that way..." He paused. "Thank you again."

With a twinkle in her eye she said, "You can thank me by helping me get these groceries put away...Your Highness."

Luke fixed the shelves for Joyce the preschool teacher the next day and went to the twins' piano recital with Marilyn the mom on Thursday afternoon. That was the end of round one, since he had already had first "dates"—at least, Annah's definition of dates—with Terri the mailcarrier, Carol the volleyball player and Shannon the nurse. It had all happened so fast he was beginning to feel like he needed a scorecard to keep them straight.

When he got off the phone with his Minister of Domestic Affairs on Thursday evening, Annah had closed up shop and was making dinner. Before you could say "God save the prince" she had him chopping up vegetables for the salad. He thought he was doing a pretty good job of it, too, although he had to keep shifting around to keep a certain feline from jumping up on the counter. As it was, the cat kept rubbing against his ankles.

"You could trip a guy that way, Beast," he said, pointing his paring knife at the cat.

"Rauw," said Purrkins, looking up at him adoringly.

"Can't we lock him up somewhere?" he asked Annah.

"How about your bedroom?"

"Funny."

"Well, we don't have a dungeon, Your Highness. Why don't you feed him? Eating ought to keep him busy for a while."

"I did feed him. He left his full bowl in the laundry room and followed me back in here."

"He wouldn't even eat? Uh-oh, he's got it bad!" Annah said, teasing.

Luke looked panicked. "Got what? Fleas?"

"Got it bad for you, Luke." She laughed. "From the talk in my shops, there's a lot of that going around."

"I hope the rest are female humans."

"You know exactly who they are."

He put the salads on the table. "I don't know. Things have gotten a little quiet around here. I was wondering what my consultant had to say."

"Well, they all asked you out the first time, except Shannon."

"So?"

"Ball's in your court, oh, princess seeker."

"Are you saying that I should ask them out now?"

"Right first try."

He thought about that for a minute. "All right," he said cautiously. "How do I go about doing that?"

She looked at him, but he was serious. "Wait a minute. Are you telling me that you've never asked a woman out?"

He frowned. "Of course I have. But generally my staff would take care of the details."

"Your staff? Whoa. Just in case you're thinking of me, think again," she told him. "I helped you out in round one. But I've got to tell you—ordinary guys do their own asking."

"And there was always some social occasion involved," he went on. "A ball, a state dinner, a diplomatic luncheon, that sort of thing."

"Well, we're a little short on highbrow social functions here at the Point this month, so that won't work. You'll just have to ask them on a regular date."

"When?"

"Soon, unless you've been given an extension on that deadline that I don't know about."

"I suppose I could fit one in on Friday afternoon and night, and Saturday afternoon and night," he said, musing.

"That's four," Annah said. "What about the other one?"

He thought about that. "That's Shannon," he said. "I think I'll just have coffee with her when she comes in here on Sunday morning. If anyone's 'got it bad,' it's not she."

"Well, don't take it personally. She's never come right out and said so, but I gather that she gave her heart away a long time ago. My guess is that she's never quite gotten over him, whoever he was."

"Would she be willing to marry someone else?"

"Who knows? Only she can decide that, but she'll need a little time. I know she likes you, Luke. She told me it was the nicest evening out with a man she's had in a long time. From her, that's something."

"Where do you think I should take the others?"

He was serious. She had to remind herself that as experienced as he no doubt was in other ways, he was a beginner in the mechanics of dating. "Why not just do something you like to do? That will give you a better idea as to whether you'd be compatible."

He looked at her as though she had just thought up the Theory of Relativity. "Great idea," he said approvingly.

She couldn't resist adding, "Beats the heck out of going up to them and asking if they'd be willing to bear your children."

He shook his head. "Just what I needed. A matchmaker who's a comedienne."

"Laughs, no extra charge."

He ended up taking Joyce for an autumn hike after she got out of nursery school the next day. That evening he escorted Carol to a concert in the next town, and on Saturday afternoon he took a harbor cruise with Marilyn and the twins. Later he and Terri went on a candlelight tour of historic homes in the area, followed by dinner.

To his surprise, the next morning at the coffee shop Shannon asked him to accompany her to the opening of an exhibit at a nearby art gallery that evening.

By Monday morning he needed a cup of Annah's coffee to get him started. Wilfred and Eldridge took up their accustomed stools on either side of him.

"Notice anything strange in town lately?" Wilfred asked his cohort.

"Ayup. Things are looking a bit different around here," replied Eldridge.

"It's Luke, here."

"Paintin' the town red."

"Ayup."

Luke said nothing. He had learned there was no need to.

"Haven't you got anything to say for yourself, young man?" Wilfred finally asked him.

Luke shrugged. "Not a crime to take a woman out on a date, is it?"

"*Five* women," Eldridge corrected him.

"And living with a sixth," added Wilfred.

"Now don't start that again," Luke warned. "Annah's told you, she and I are—"

"*Friends.*" Eldridge gave a snort. "In my day, we had another name for it when a man and woman shared a house—"

"Who hadn't entered into the bonds of holy matrimony," finished Wilfred.

Luke caught Annah's eye. She shrugged and grinned, clearly enjoying seeing him get this undeserved comeuppance. *You can't win,* she mouthed.

She was right, so Luke drank his coffee and tried to ignore the byplay. They ended by exonerating him, but only because Annah was above reproach.

"As to what you're up to, giving them other five the rush…"

"We want to know what your intentions—"

Luke turned to one and then the other. "Jealous, gentlemen?"

That got them. They got all ruffled and flustered about that for a while.

"Just wait until you see us in action on the dance floor—" Wilfred sputtered.

"At the Firehouse Dance," Eldridge finished.

"Show a whippersnapper like you a thing or two about courtin'."

"Won't be a woman over fifty who won't be all atwitter."

Eventually, they settled down and decided that if Annah said Luke was all right, then the young women in town could take care of themselves. Annah said that he was, and they left, still muttering to each other on the way out.

Still, they had brought up a point that was bothering Luke. "Do you think the women are wondering why I'm dating five of them at once?" he asked Annah while she cleaned up after closing.

"Maybe wondering, but I don't think minding," she answered. "It's not like you're sneaking around or anything. You're being very up-front about it. And remember, these women are available, but they're not hard up."

"So you think it's okay if I take some more time and keep testing the waters with them?"

She gave him a knowing grin. "Why ever not, Luke? It's just exactly what they're doing with you."

After dropping Marilyn off Thursday night, Luke pulled into the driveway behind Annah's car. He hadn't liked borrowing hers, so he had rented a car for the remainder of his stay. She had wanted him to get an ordinary sedan, but he had insisted that an ordinary guy could drive the quintessential American sports car. It was a great date car, plus he liked taking it for drives along the coast when he had some free time. Good think time. Not that it had yielded much. Another round of dates that week had brought Luke no closer to being able to decide between the five.

He stretched behind the wheel. It felt good to be home. And it hadn't taken long to start thinking of Annah's house as home. He could relax there. And he liked knowing Annah was there, although she was careful to give him his space. No postdate reporting, unless he wanted to talk to her. Tonight he was earlier than he had expected, and he was happy to see that the downstairs lights were on.

Not only that, he realized as he put his key in the back door lock. There was music playing. Loud music. He entered the kitchen and was under immediate assault by Purrkins, who rubbed back and forth against his legs enthusiastically. Either the damn cat had radar, or he knew the sound of a great car engine—even over the sound of Annah's music. After stooping to give him a cursory pat on the head, Luke went into the living room with his feline shadow following.

Annah was dancing to the music, dust cloth in hand, with her back to the doorway. It wasn't the way her mother had done it, but her favorite way to clean was to crank up something good and fast, good and loud. She figured she'd be finished and in bed long before Luke came home from his date.

But she'd figured wrong. She spun around and bumped into him, standing in the doorway. He caught her and, without missing a beat, started dancing her around the living room. She went along with him, caught up in the spontaneity of it. That was new, from him. She loved it. Suddenly she started to laugh.

"What's so funny?" he asked her over the music, not missing a step.

"This," she said between breaths, giving the dust cloth that was clutched between their hands a shake. "Cinderella, dancing with the prince."

"What prince?" he asked, looking around. "Me, I'm just an ordinary guy."

Not true, she knew. It felt extraordinarily good, being silly with him. She was still laughing when the song was over, collapsed against him. But the next cut was a slow one. Not looking at him, she pushed away and went over and turned off the CD player. "Not a very good song for cleaning," she said lightly, then bent over to dust the coffee table.

"I'll take your word for it," he said, backing up a step. He knew that if she hadn't turned off the music, he would have her in his arms right now. And he wasn't sure how he felt about that.

She gave him a tiny grin. "You mean this isn't the way cleaning is done in your palace?" she asked.

"If it was, I'd never know it. Such work is done when I'm not around. All I know is that it's always clean." He paused and then observed, "It must be hard for you, doing all this on top of running two businesses. Could I help, while I'm staying here?"

Help clean? The prince? Before she could answer he added, "I'd be happy to hire a maid service."

"Thanks, but to tell the truth, I've never wanted one. I like keeping house," she said. "Of course, the fun part is decorating it. I just redid the upstairs before you arrived. Dusting's not my favorite activity, but it is an excuse to pick up my things and think about what makes them special to me."

Luke watched her. He had never met anyone who

took such joy in the little things in life. Most of his life was spent in contact with the ultrarich, ultrapowerful, ultrabored. How that jaded crowd would laugh at Annah's simple revelation! But he found it endearing.

Which was reason enough to get himself up the stairs and her out of his sight.

Chapter Six

"So you're the young man who's been stealing hearts around here."

When he came in to help Annah move some heavy racks in her secondhand shop the next day, Luke hadn't been expecting a full house—much less to be greeted in such a way. The other faces in the crowd looked familiar, but he didn't recognize the speaker, a plump woman with white hair and clear blue eyes.

He wasn't quite sure how to react to her words, so he introduced himself. "You must be mistaking me for someone else, ma'am. I don't believe we've met," he said easily. "I'm Luke Hansson."

"You're the one all right. The one who's trying to take my baby away from me."

While Luke tried to figure out which of the women he was dating she belonged to, she broke into a wide grin. "I'm Louise Cartelli," she said. "Purrkins' mama."

As if on cue the cat appeared at his feet, looking up at him longingly, and gave a plaintive, "Rauw."

The woman laughed out loud. "I see I came back to get him not a moment too soon," she said, picking up the cat and snuggling him against her bosom.

"Pleased to meet you," Luke said. "And I'm sorry about your sister."

A sheen of tears brightened the twinkle in her eyes. "Ah, well, we all have losses, and we deal with them as well as the good Lord lets us. Me, I take consolation in being in the company of my good friends and neighbors," she said, looking around the room. "And they've been telling me that my kitty isn't the only one in Anders Point who wants to snuggle up with you."

While the other women in the room laughed at that, Luke shot a help-me glance at Annah, who was coming out of her office with an armload of clothes. "Hi, Luke," she said warmly, oblivious to his predicament. "It'll be a few minutes until I can start that project with you. Do you mind waiting?"

"Not at all," he said. "I'll be right outside, whenever you need me."

"Now, don't be silly, boy. It's colder than a meat locker out there," said Mrs. Cartelli, still chuckling.

"I don't mind the cold," Luke said. There wasn't a man alive who wouldn't choose to brave an Arctic blast without a coat rather than stay in a small enclosed place with one woman making sport of him and a group of her allies looking on.

"Likely not, when you've got 'em lined up waiting to take Purrkins' place warming your bed," she said, chuckling. "Not that any of the five of 'em would do it, mind you. Not without a ring on her finger. I've known 'em all since they was in diapers. They're good girls, every one. They'd all make fine wives.''

"If I'm ever looking for one, I'll remember that," he said, instinctively trying to throw this grandmotherly bloodhound off his trail. "But right now we're just friends." He hoped that catch-all American phrase would put an end to the conversation.

"Oh-*ho!* That's what you said, didn't you, Lynn?"

"Sure did," a very pregnant woman said with a grin.

"Me, too," added a woman who was looking at coats for the two little boys who were chasing each other around her legs.

"Annah will set him straight, just like she set you straight," Mrs. Cartelli pronounced. "Her and that no-fail true-love insight of hers."

Luke decided it was time to put someone else in the hot seat. "Do you mean to tell me Annah's never been wrong? Ever?"

"Never known to be, not in this town," declared Mrs. Cartelli. "And believe me, she's had plenty of chances. Everyone consults her before they tie the knot. You will too, if you've got as much brains as you've got brawn."

Annah chimed in, "Right now, it's his brawn I need."

"Well, I'd best be moving along, anyway. Got to get the house warmed up again," Mrs. Cartelli said. "Thanks to both of you for watching my baby for me."

"You're welcome," Annah told her. "But Luke did most of the work."

"No problem," Luke added, carefully using another American phrase he'd learned. He said it casually, but was surprised to realize that he meant it. "Bye."

Purrkins gave him one last longing glance over Mrs.

Cartelli's shoulder as she carried him out the door. "Rauw," he replied mournfully.

When he got home later on, no furry feline was waiting at the door to greet him. Luke had to admit he missed the little guy—sort of the way a kid missed a loose tooth that finally fell out. When you lost something familiar—annoying though it might be—it left a gap in your life.

Annah wasn't home that night, either. The youth business group for which she served as a mentor was having a spaghetti supper at the high school as a fundraiser. Luke filled up on the stew she had left for him, but the house seemed so empty that he decided to go out for a drive. Content as he was on one level, the restlessness was still there inside him, and growing. He needed to be going somewhere—anywhere. He drove for a long time, farther than he had originally intended. But in the end he found himself back at Annah's.

She was still awake. "Hi," she greeted him, coming out of the coffee shop. "I just finished getting the baking ready for tomorrow morning. Where have you been?"

"Driving."

"Are you hungry?"

He shouldn't be, after the dinner he had eaten, but she seemed to have some kind of intuition about this. She always asked him that at the right moment. And he loved being asked. He loved being *fed*, by her. It seemed he couldn't get enough of Annah's cooking, which made it a good thing that some of the local men had asked him to play hockey with them a couple of nights a week. Serious skating helped burn off serious eating.

"I could use a bite," he told her. "What did you have in mind?"

"I like to have a cup of hot chocolate before bed on a cold night like this," she said.

It sounded wonderful. He stood and watched her as she got out the ingredients. "I keep packets on hand for an emergency," she said. "But I really like it better made from scratch."

"Me, too," he said appreciatively.

She laughed. "Your Highness, I'll bet you've never had hot chocolate made from a mix in your entire life."

"Annah Lane, I haven't had hot chocolate of any kind since I was a boy."

That stopped her for a moment. "Not the drink of choice in society, is it?"

"Not a chance." He rested his hand on the counter next to her. "Got any cookies to go with that?" he asked, his voice coming from close to her ear.

"Just made some. Check the jar." Annah was relieved when he went over to do just that. Living in the house with him for two weeks had done nothing to dilute her reaction to him. When he got close, she melted like the chocolate she was putting into the warm milk on the stove.

He took the lid off of the chunky earthenware jar. "Mmm," he said, chewing. "What kind are these?"

"Sugar cookies," she told him, once again amazed that he didn't know such a simple thing.

"They're...mmm," he said again, biting into another one.

She handed him a plate. "How about putting some out for us to have with our hot chocolate, while there are still some left?"

They sat companionably at her little drop-leaf table,

eating and drinking in near darkness—only the light over the stove was on. It struck Luke at that moment that he was happy, for no particular reason. Such moments were coming closer together since he'd moved in here. Or perhaps he was getting better at appreciating them.

Annah watched him, thinking that he bore little resemblance to the impatient royal who had paced her coffee shop just two weeks earlier. Becoming an ordinary man had mellowed him out some. Still, tension ran not far under his surface, and she knew that the deadline was never far from his conscious mind.

"How is it going, Luke?" she asked softly.

He knew what she meant, without her having to spell it out. He set his mug down. "I don't know," he answered honestly. "I'm really not sure where things should be at this point."

"Where are things?"

He shrugged. "There's not much daylight between them," he said. "They're all nice, hometown women, but I think they'd handle the public role of being my princess all right. And they all seem to love kids. Whether they want to have them, though—that's a delicate subject."

"Yes, it is," Annah agreed quietly.

"I mean, it's not exactly the kind of thing that a man brings up with a woman that he is just dating casually. Are women more open with other women about that kind of thing?"

"Most are," Annah said truthfully. "At least, these women have been with me. As I told you, Shannon is desperate to have a baby. And Marilyn has said she'd like to have more before the twins get too much older."

"How about the other three? They're all interested in their careers."

"Well, I know for a fact that each of those women would quit their jobs in a minute for the chance to get married and raise a family."

Those women. But not her, Luke thought. What made Annah so different, so set against having babies? He stood up and went to the window.

She stood up too. "Luke? What's the matter?"

He shook off that last thought of Annah and concentrated on the five women who were eligible to be his bride. "What could be wrong? Thanks to you, my situation has changed dramatically in two weeks. Now I have my choice of five women, any one of whom would make a suitable bride."

"But," she prodded.

"They're just what I said I wanted."

"But…"

"Somehow it still feels like there's something missing," he admitted at last, turning to face her.

"What something?"

"I'm not sure. I feel that they're compatible, but—" He stopped, frowning.

Annah thought she knew what he meant, even if he didn't. She knew compatibility wasn't enough, but he wasn't ready to admit that yet. If there was something more between him and any of these women, there should be some sparks. That was always the first sign her true-love instinct gave her. She wondered how she could ask him about the physical side of things. *So, Your Highness, have you been getting any?* just didn't seem subtle enough. And she didn't want to know the answer to that, anyway.

"Are you sure you're giving it enough of a chance?" she asked instead.

"What do you mean?" He started pacing. "I've been out with each of them three times, haven't I?"

His sudden defensiveness was telling. "I was just wondering if you—" She stopped. "This is awkward, to be asking this."

He stood in front of her. "Asking what?"

"Asking whether there have been any sparks."

"Sparks?" He frowned down at her. "What are you talking about, Annah?"

"Have you...gotten physical at all?"

She had a feeling she struck a nerve. "Now there's one hell of a question," he growled, as he resumed pacing.

"I told you it was."

"It's not really anyone's business. Not even yours." Especially not hers, he thought, though not knowing why.

"No, it isn't," she agreed. "I was just trying to help. If you don't want to tell me, that's fine."

"I mean," he continued, "I'm not the kind to kiss and tell, and these women aren't the kind you mess around with. They're women I'm considering marrying! They're the kind of women who'd make good mothers." What did she expect—that they'd be shedding clothes for him at his mere glance, like the women in his old life did?

"Luke, it's okay, really," she said. "It's just that an ordinary man would have gotten around to kissing a woman by the third—"

"Who says I haven't?" he said, squaring off in front of her. That one had made a direct hit on his ego. "As a matter of fact, Miss Nosy Matchmaker, I've kissed all of them.''

She stood her ground, looking him in the eye. "And?"

"And nothing," he growled. "I took them home. I kissed them. I said good-night. I left. I've been a perfect gentleman."

That was it, Annah thought. He was holding back. How was he ever going to find out who was right for him if he didn't give it a chance? "Maybe it's the way you're doing it," she suggested gently.

That got him. She had been taking jabs long enough, and his ego could only stand so much before fighting back. "Is that what you think?" he said. "Well, then, I'll *show* you."

He yanked her against him, no gentleman now. With a swift, sure motion he covered her mouth with his and boldly thrust his tongue inside her parted lips. Swallowing her gasp of astonishment, he backed her up against the wall, sealing his hips against hers and plunging his tongue expertly into the warm depths of her. He felt her initial surprise dissolve like sugar on his tongue, and she moved against him, welcoming his exploration. Something exploded inside him. *Sparks?* More like fireworks.

After starving for him for so long, now that she had finally gotten a taste of him she couldn't get enough. She lifted her arms around his neck, savoring the weight of his very-masculine body as he leaned against her, the rippling warmth that radiated from every point of contact. It was as if she had never kissed a man before, never been kissed. And she hadn't—not like this. Her prince kissed like a pirate bent on plunder. He seemed to know instinctively what to do to heat her up to dangerously new levels, and his reaction to even the least little move on her part told her that he was going there with her. *Holding back?* Not now. Not with her.

Oh, sweet heaven. *Not* with her.

She wedged her hands against the solid muscle of his chest and gave a push. It wasn't really enough to budge him, but he lifted his head and stepped away from her. Her legs were shaking—shaking!—as she leaned there against the wall. And shaken was how she felt; from her skin that was still tingling, all the way to her core; shaken by the sheer magnitude of that kiss.

It took all of his strength for Luke to exert control over his body, which was clearly of the opinion that losing control was the way to go. What had come over him? It had started out as a mere kiss, just to show her, but the kiss had fueled some kind of chemical reaction. Nothing at all like the platonic kisses he'd shared with his bride candidates.

It was no doubt fueled by the closeness of sharing her house, he thought. Here she was under his nose, using the shower right before he did, dressing and undressing in the room down the hall, slipping between the sheets and stretching out that beautiful body on her bed.... Yeah, he'd been thinking about her like that. Okay, he was super aware of her—but what normal male wouldn't be, under the circumstances? He swore beneath his breath, knowing full well that proximity was only part of it. He also happened to find Annah extremely attractive—small wonder that he was attracted to her. This kiss was a natural expression of his lust, he told himself. Why did he always feel it for the wrong women?

He looked at her watching him, her full lips trembling as she drew in shaky breaths. Wrong woman or not, he had the tremendous urge to pull her back into his arms. But then he remembered that she had been the one to pull away. No matter how she had responded to him during the kiss, no matter what his hormones were urging him to do now, he respected that.

So what should he do? The situation was awkward in the extreme. There was no point asking her whether she still thought there was something wrong with the way he kissed. She'd already taken that accusation back with her own lips. Similarly there was no point in apologizing to someone who had practically asked for his kiss and then fully participated in it. He had stopped when she had wanted to, and now the kiss was over. As a gentleman, there were only two things he could do, one of which he had already done five times that week.

"Good night," he said. And he left the room.

Then he did something he hadn't had to do the other times. Went straight into the shower and turned it all the way to C.

Annah paced back and forth across her secondhand store. She ran a hand through the hair she had just arranged, messing it up again. She caught herself about to bite a nail and stopped just in time. What was wrong with her? She was never edgy like this. She was calm, serene, able to handle anything that came up in her life.

Catching a glimpse of herself in the mirror, she stopped and took a good look. *Liar*, the Annah in the mirror seemed to say.

She turned away and started to straighten up the racks before opening, but before she knew it she was pacing again. This was Luke's fault. She had been increasingly restless ever since he had arrived. His presence in her life had shattered her hard-won tranquillity. It wasn't just last night's kiss—although that had certainly compounded the problem. This went way deeper than the chemical attraction between them, and that in and of itself was considerable. He had also sparked an emotional restlessness that swirled around inside her, dredging up flotsam from her past that she had let settle to the bottom. While it had lain undisturbed, she had been at peace. Now she had to deal with it again, and with him. Darn that man! Since she couldn't have him, at least she wanted her serenity back.

Something else had surfaced along with the painful memories, something even more threatening. It was her old dream, the one she thought she had jettisoned for good. After her divorce she had resigned herself to a life without love and a family. She had told herself that she didn't want that anymore. But now she couldn't believe herself. She *did* still want it—even though for her, it was an impossible dream.

It had kept her out of the running as a potential bride for the prince from the beginning, and she had accepted that. But back then she hadn't yet shared her lonely house with Luke, whose presence now seemed to fill it up—like he seemed to fill her up. Back then she hadn't cooked for him, laughed with him, danced with him, waited until the end of a long day to share good news with him. She hadn't begun to feel the warmth that he kept well hidden or the heat of knowing he was sleeping under her roof or the fire of his kiss. How easy it was to get caught up in the wonder of it all! It was like being married, yet not like the marriage she had known. It was too good—and too good to be true.

She pulled back the curtain and got a view into the

driveway next door where Luke was helping a group of middle school boys with their basketball shots. She swallowed the lump that formed in her throat. This was the worst part. In the beginning she hadn't yet seen him with kids of all ages: with these boys; with Marilyn's twins, who adored him; with the little ones in Joyce's nursery school. Prince or not, he would be a great father. And he wanted to be one, so badly.

That's why, hard to resist as Luke was, resist him she must. Because what he wanted most from a woman, she couldn't give him.

When Luke came in from shooting hoops with the kids next door, Annah was at work in her secondhand shop. Saturday afternoons were her busiest time, he knew.

He got the milk out of the fridge and stopped himself from taking a swig right out of the carton. As he poured himself a glass, he marveled at that. At his palace he had never had to fend for himself in the kitchen. Drinking milk from the carton was a real ordinary-guy thing.

And stopping from doing it was a *married*-guy thing.

He walked through Annah's house with his glass— not the business part, but the private part of the house, the part that was hers and hers alone. He now thought of its smallness as cozy. He found it hard to walk through the living room without sitting down at the window seat or on one of the comfy love seats that faced each other by the hearth, inviting conversation. She had made the pillows and plumped them herself, and she always kept a stack of wood at the ready by the fireplace. There was no television. He knew she had a small one in her bedroom, but he had never known her to turn it on. Her CD player sat on a bookshelf whose contents were as varied in reading material as in musical selections. Here on the coffee table were her gardening magazines and the novel she was currently reading. He picked it up and paged through it. Small print, big words. Annah was no intellectual lightweight.

Her small dining room smelled richly of furniture wax, and the antique table in the middle of it gleamed. The cabinet off to the side was stocked with her craft things. Right now she had a half-completed sweater in the basket she carried around with her to work on during her spare moments. He lifted it up carefully. It looked almost finished, but not big enough to fit her. She was knitting a sweater for a child, he realized. He wondered who.

Annah's signature room, though, was the kitchen. From the gingham curtains she had made herself, to the spotless countertops, to the much-used copper-bottom pots, Luke felt at home. And he got hungry every time he walked in here. There was almost always something cooking—stew on the stove, bread in the machine, a cake in the oven. And that didn't count the early-morning baking she did for the coffee shop, which created the aromas he had been waking up to for the past weeks.

She really was amazing. She ran a home and two businesses without a fuss—and then there was her volunteer work: coordinating refreshments for the Firehouse Dance, teaching church school, serving as a mentor in the youth business cooperative in town.

How did she do it all? Her full, busy life was a striking contrast to that of the idle rich he came into contact with in his royal life. And it was in direct opposition to that of the woman he had grown up with.

Even as a boy, he had known his mother to be vain,
superficial and self-serving. He felt for his warm and
patient father, who had married her for the sake of the
unity of his country—her father had been threatening
rebellion. Their marriage had been an empty shell, and
he a product of it only because his mother had been
required to produce an heir. The fact that there were
no other children after him was no accident. His mother
had taken to her suite of rooms and run the social life
of the palace until she had died, while Luke was away
at college. His father had kept a firm hold of the country itself, but his life had been a lonely one for a man
of such warmth. Luke and he had been very close. His
recent death had been a real blow.

What would his father say to him now? Luke had a
feeling he would approve of the kind of marriage his
son was looking for, so different from his own. Luke
didn't want a cold life for him and for his children. He
wanted a woman who would warm up the palace and
make it a real home, like Annah had made her house
a home.

There he was, back to Annah, who really had nothing to do with this. Talk in the coffee shop was that
she had opened her businesses with her divorce settlement. He didn't know why her marriage had ended,
but it seemed clear that Annah was living the life of
her choice.

What about the five women he was dating? They
each juggled careers with home life. Their houses each
had their own personal touch, too. He didn't feel as at
home in theirs as in Annah's, but that must be because
he had spent so much time here. Living here was like
being married.

For a moment he let himself wonder what it would

be like to be married to Annah. It wasn't just how he felt here in the downstairs of her home. After that kiss he'd done a lot of thinking about what it would be like upstairs, in bed. With the kind of chemistry they had, they just might burn down the house. But, he reminded himself, a woman's having the ability to fire up his libido wasn't on his list of requirements for a potential bride. He didn't need fireworks—just a loving woman to warm his bed, one that wanted to have his children.

The sexual connection he made with Annah was just a dead-end street. He'd been there before, and he wasn't about to get involved with a woman who didn't want children. *Babies aren't my thing,* she had said, and he would be wise to remind himself of that. Often.

Just then, he heard a baby crying. It sounded like it was coming from the secondhand shop. He set his empty glass down on the kitchen counter and opened the door that led to the hallway. There he paused. In the back room, he could see Annah. She was all alone, except for the infant she held in her arms.

"Mommy will be right back," she crooned, swaying gently back and forth as she cradled the baby against her. "She forgot your bottle, but it won't take her long to get it. I'll take good care of you until she gets back."

Luke felt something give him a swift boot in the gut, and his insides shook as he watched. The woman he was watching was the picture of maternal care. She hummed and stroked and rocked the baby into comfort, while he stood spellbound. Whether it was instinct or practice, he didn't know, but there was no doubt that Annah Lane knew exactly what she was doing. Not only that. There was an expression of bliss on her face as she nuzzled the tiny, fuzzy head with her lips.

It didn't make sense, what he was seeing before him.

His gut was telling him one thing, but he just couldn't rationalize it. How could she be so good with babies and say they weren't her thing?

That was it. *Her* thing. Apparently she was perfectly content to enjoy an occasional cuddle with someone else's baby, even though she didn't want one herself. The picture he was seeing before him was enchanting, but deceptively so. His gut was steering him wrong again.

As he stepped backward through the doorway, his movement must have caught her eye. She turned and looked at him over her little bundle, her hand carefully supporting the baby's head. But no sooner had their gazes met than he closed the door between them.

Chapter Seven

Luke just didn't have time to figure Annah out, and it was none of his business, anyway. It aggravated him that each date with another woman only made him want her more. It was a cruel longing, and a patient one. It resisted his every effort to turn it off, and that was starting to wear on him. His next round of dates went by almost in a blur, until he dragged himself into the house on Wednesday evening after hockey.

At the sound of the back door opening, Annah turned from the stove where she was warming up a pot of potato soup for a late dinner. She had been keeping her distance from Luke, physically and emotionally, ever since that kiss. But one look at his face, white and drawn, had her over to his side in an instant.

"Luke, what's wrong?" she asked, looking up at him anxiously. "You look awful!"

"Thanks." He tried for a grin, but it came out more like a grimace.

"Did you get hurt at the rink?"

"Nope," he said, sinking into a chair. "Just feel lousy."

On a whim, she put a hand to his forehead. "Luke, you feel like you've got a fever," she said, her voice rising. "I'm calling the doctor."

"No," he said, his tone reminding her of a fact she forgot now and then—that he was the ruler of a country. "I just need some sleep. I'm going up to bed."

He scraped the chair back and heaved himself out of it. Then he held the edge of the table for a second or two, as if for balance.

"Do you want me to bring your soup up?" she called after him as he headed for the stairs.

He shook his head.

Annah had never known him to turn down food of any kind, and her potato soup was one of his favorites. He must really be sick. Panic seized her. He was a world leader, she reminded herself. His health was vital. If anything happened to him—well, not while he was staying with her it wouldn't! She snatched up the phone. He had forbidden her to call a doctor, but he hadn't said anything about a nurse.

Ten minutes later, Annah let Shannon in the back door. "I've never seen him like this," she said worriedly.

"I've never seen *you* like this," Shannon replied, giving her a curious look. "You were more calm in the delivery room."

"That was normal and natural. You were there and everything was okay with Drew. And I was helping her take those big breaths. They calmed me down, too."

"Well, take one now and tell me what's wrong with Luke. I'm trying to figure out why you called me, since it's a pretty safe bet he's not in labor."

Annah held her breath for moment and exhaled slowly. That was better. "He's sick. I think he has a fever," she said. "He wouldn't let me call the doctor, but I figured you could tell me whether I ought to be packing him off to the emergency room."

"I'm not sure I'll be much help, but I'll have a look at him."

Annah took her upstairs to Luke's bedroom. He did not look happy with her. "Maybe it's best if I left," she said, edging her way out of the room.

A few minutes later Shannon called her back in.

"I was just telling Luke that it sure looks like he's picked up the bug that's been making the rounds around town," she said. "You know what to watch out for, Annah. Otherwise, just give it a little time—rest, fluids, you know the drill."

She turned to Luke. "I'm putting you in Annah's care, and you couldn't be in better hands. She was a real natural in the delivery room."

Luke was trying to grasp the conversation, but his head was swimming. "But babies," he said, fighting back waves of dizziness, "aren't Annah's—" He stopped, trying to garner his concentration.

"Do you know what he's talking about?" Shannon asked Annah.

Annah bent down next to Luke. "Shannon means that I was Drew's labor coach when she had Lexi," she told him.

"Lexi? You mean Whit's daughter Lexi?"

"Yes."

"Sweet li'l girl. Told Whit he's a lucky bastard."

"How does Luke know Prince Whit?" Shannon asked curiously.

"Uh…as a matter of fact, they've spoken on the

phone, when Drew has called me,'' Annah improvised quickly, steering her out of the room. Which was true, as far as it went.

"Sounds like they hit it off pretty well."

Annah shrugged. "Guys," she said.

Her one-word explanation seemed to cover it for Shannon, who left soon after. But before she did, she said to Annah, "I don't know if Luke has told you or not, but we're not seeing each other anymore."

"You're *not?*" That was news to Annah, who blurted out, "Why not?"

Shannon gave a crooked little smile. "Just not meant to be," she said. "I believe there's only one right person for each of us. I already found mine."

And then lost him, Annah thought, but respected Shannon's right to keep her story to herself.

Shannon was looking at her. "After tonight, though, I'm wondering whether I'm the only one who has."

Annah made up a tray and took it upstairs later. At first she thought Luke was dozing, but he opened his eyes when she stepped into his bedroom.

"I was just bringing you a few things you might want during the night," she said. "Something to bring the fever down if you want it, some juice, water, a washcloth. Is there anything else I can get for you?"

"No, thanks." He still felt a little woozy, but it was better if he kept still. "Is Shannon still here?"

"No. She left me on duty."

A vague memory of something he'd said teased his mind. "I almost blew it, didn't I?"

"The way you talked about Whit? Almost." Annah sat in the chair next to his bed. "Don't worry about Shannon, though. She'd be the last person to say anything if she suspected who you really are. I've never heard her repeat gossip, much less start it.''

''She's out of the running.''

''So she told me.''

''You were right, Annah,'' he went on. He felt like he was babbling, but he kept talking to keep her there. He liked having her there in the room with him; liked the soothing sound of her voice. ''I couldn't compete with that guy from her past.''

''Don't take it personally.''

''Nah. We all have ghosts of our own.''

Another woman might have asked about his, but this was Annah. He loved her for not asking. It made him want to tell her.

''I suppose we all do,'' was all she said. Then she stood up.

''No. Don't go,'' he said.

''I don't want to impose. There's nothing else I can really do for you.''

''Stay and talk to me. No one's ever done this for me before.''

It hit her right in the soft underbelly, the knowledge that with all he had at his command, he was still lonely. ''Not even when you were sick as a boy?''

''Oh, a nurse was always posted outside the door, and my father slipped away to see me whenever his duties permitted it, but I didn't have anyone who would stay and keep me company like this.''

''What about your mother?''

''Least of all my mother. Kids weren't her thing.'' He hadn't meant to, but when he heard himself say it, it sounded like an echo of what she had told him. ''But you're not like that,'' he added hastily. ''You're here.''

Annah hardly noticed what he said last. She was

busy picturing a lonely little boy growing up in a palace full of treasure but empty of love. No wonder he was looking for a good mother for his children! Everybody needed mothering in their life, not the smothering kind, but the positive, nurturing kind. Apparently Luke had gone through his life running on empty.

She moved over to the bed. He noticed how she took care to sit down gently so as not to jar him. Ever so softly, she took his hand in hers. "You're going to do it, you know," she told him determinedly. "You're going to find the right woman to love you and your children."

"I don't know. It's getting harder instead of easier. They're all so evenly matched." Her hand felt wonderful in his. He pulled it up under his cheek, to hold her there.

The rasp of his evening whiskers against the back of her hand sent a thrill racing through her. "You're not still thinking in terms of your requirements, are you? Surely you have another way to differentiate between them after all this time."

"Like what?" He wanted to keep her talking, so he could keep hearing the sound of her voice.

"Like your feelings. They'll point you in the right direction."

"I don't think so," he said positively.

"How do you know, if you don't trust them? Luke, you won't let yourself fall in love."

"Been there, done that." The casual American phrase she'd used about her marriage was out before he realized he'd said it, slipped right over his guard, which was down, anyway.

He could hear the surprise in her voice. "You've been in love? When?"

"A long time ago. When I was too young to know better."

"What happened?"

He started to shrug, but the movement went right to his head again. He closed his eyes. "She didn't love me back."

"She *told* you that?"

He loved how she sounded indignant, for his sake. "Nope. Found out for myself, by accident."

That had been the really fun part, overhearing her phone conversation with a friend on the day they had planned to make their engagement public. *Children?* the woman he thought he loved had said, and then she had laughed. *Heavens, no. What would I do with children?... There are ways to prevent that, darling, without His Highness's ever knowing.... Without children, I'll be next in line for the throne....*

Annah's soft voice called him back to the present. "Luke, what happened?"

He opened his eyes again and tried to focus on her face. He saw concern there, and empathy. "Got my ring back," he told her simply.

"Ring? You mean you were *engaged?*"

"Not publicly. Found out a few hours before the announcement."

She muttered something under her breath. He had never heard Annah swear, and he was curious to know whether that was what she was doing. He was about to ask her when she said, "Then what?"

"Nothing." Nothing but a whole lot of hurt and anger. That had faded, but not his fierce determination that it would never, ever happen again. "So you can see why I'm not such a big fan of love."

He released her hand and closed his eyes again. She

studied him: the way his eyelashes fanned his cheeks, the way the masculine planes of his face were shadowed by a day's beard growth, the way his breathing gradually got slower and deeper. When she was sure he had fallen asleep, she stroked her hand across his forehead. Then she spoke softly.

"Luke, don't give up on love. It's still out there for you. What you felt for that woman was unrequited love. That doesn't mean it wasn't real, or wasn't painful, but it's not the same thing as true love. Give your feelings another try. Trust in what they tell you. And when they tell you that you've found the one you truly love, trust that she'll love you, too." She brushed a kiss across his forehead. "That's the way love works."

When she turned for one last look before she left, she thought she saw his eyelids flutter. But after waiting a few minutes more, she told herself she must have imagined it. And so she left him, peacefully sleeping.

Annah didn't know what had awakened her, but in the middle of the night she found herself sitting straight up in bed, heart drumming. The next instant she remembered Luke and threw back her bedclothes. Without even throwing a robe over her nightgown, she slipped into his room.

He was moving restlessly, and in the moonlight through the window she saw his eyes open and focus on her. She filled a glass from the pitcher and held it out to him. "Water?" she asked.

He took it from her and set it back on the night table, then grabbed her outstretched hand. "Woman," he replied succinctly, and pulled her into bed with him.

It never occurred to her to feel threatened. This wasn't a sexual thing. Once again in his hour of need he was turning to her, this time for comfort. Once again she felt deeply gratified. If he needed her, here she was.

He pulled her right against him, enfolding her in his arms, and she didn't resist. She snuggled her back into the curve of his body, a perfect fit. It had been oh, so long since she had shared a bed with a man. And Luke—Luke was a cuddler. He might have been sick, but she was the one who felt comforted and protected, safe in the circle of his arms. Safe from the real world, and the real things that meant she wouldn't be the wife who would get to sleep in his arms every night. His breathing was deep and regular, and in his sleep he slipped his hand under her gown. It was big and warm, and he spread it over her bare belly possessively. As comfort wrapped around her, Annah felt herself slowly drifting toward her dreams.

Luke came half-awake at dawn. Instinctively he reached out on both sides of himself, but came up empty. He was alone in the bed.

But he hadn't been all night, he knew. He'd had an angel beside him. Her soft scent still lingered, as did the impression her head had made on the usually empty pillow next to his. Annah had accepted his invitation, had slept in his arms. And during the night his narrow world had expanded. Satisfaction now spread throughout him. He stretched luxuriously and noticed that the movement didn't make his head swirl dizzily. His angel had healed him during the night. He was better. Everything was better. He slept.

Hours later he woke again, this time to the smell of cinnamon toast and the sound of his growling stomach. The note Annah had propped up on the tray said:

''Thought you might be hungry.'' And she was right, as usual. He sat up and ate every crumb of the toast and washed it down with tea, warm from the pot, feeling his strength return with each bite.

He set the tray aside and swung his legs over the side of the bed experimentally. After a moment he got to his feet; just a bit shaky. That was good enough for him, and he headed across the hall into the bathroom.

The shower felt good: nice and warm and invigorating. He stood under the spray a long time, letting his body revive and his insights flow. The signals coming from his gut were strong and clear. *You've found her, Luke! She's the one you've been looking for. She's the one!*

But when he stood in the chill air, toweling off and dressing, his intellect was in its cold, harsh element and pressed its advantage. *Have you gone mad? The past has proven that you can't trust your feelings. And you've heard from her own mouth that she can't be the one. Listen, fool! Use your brain—and choose someone else.*

The two sides battled it out for the rest of the day, which he spent in one of the love seats that framed the fireplace, ostensibly doing the paperwork that his staff could not attend to in his stead. He had the house to himself. Annah was helping out at the big Thanksgiving dinner given yearly in the basement of the town hall for—well, for whoever needed it that year, was the way they put it.

Luke had canceled his own plans to have the holiday dinner with Marilyn's whole family at the home of her parents, saying he didn't want the twins to catch whatever he'd had. In truth, he was relieved not to be going. After what had happened between him and Annah, he wasn't sure he had it in him to go through the motions of playing the attentive suitor to another woman. All he knew was that time was marching mercilessly toward his deadline. In just a little over two weeks was the Firehouse Dance, his day of reckoning.

Work was supposed to help take his mind off of his situation, but among his papers he found an updated rundown on the plans for his wedding. Arrangements had of course been made, because of the timing. Virtually everything was in place on the Constellation Isles now, from every item on the menu to the wedding rings handmade by the finest craftswoman in a country renowned for its jewelry. Everything except for the bride he had yet to choose.

He shunted the plans aside and reached for some official documents that awaited his approval. But he seemed to have lost his characteristic ability to focus on the task at hand and at last had to set those papers aside, also. His mind was preoccupied, and it was just as well. He had a lot of sorting out to do about Annah, and logic told him that the more time he spent considering both sides of the issue, the sooner he'd find the right answer.

When Annah returned, they shared a Thanksgiving dinner of leftover potato soup. During the meal, she told him about the meal in the town hall, who was there, what was said. While she talked, he tried not to look too deeply into her eyes, tried not to become mesmerized by the sound of her voice, tried not to let her smile bewitch him. His intellect was right. She seemed to be the right woman for him in every way but one, and that one was enough to override everything. His feelings were strong, but they were wrong.

After dinner he returned to sit by the fire, and she took the love seat opposite him. She had her knitting with her, and settled down to work. He picked up his paperwork again, although the effort was futile. His mind refused to focus on the pages before him. Finally he gave up and just stared into the fire.

Annah watched him out of the corner of her eye. She wondered if he had any memory of the night before, of sleeping beside her. Probably not, she decided. He hadn't let on that he had at all, treating her the same way he always did at dinner. True, he had seemed even more quiet than usual, but maybe he wasn't feeling as well as he had told her he was. Most likely in his memory the night had been lost in the blur of fever. In hers, however, it was indelible. She would never forget how it had felt to be held in his arms, but neither would she ever mention it to him. Like she had with the kiss, she could tuck it away to be brought out later, when he was married and gone. If he couldn't be hers to have and to hold, she would have that to remember and cherish.

The sound of his voice snapped her out of her thoughts. "Who's the sweater for?" he asked.

Annah noticed that she had let her knitting drop to her lap, forgotten. "It's for a nine-year-old homeless girl. The shelter a few towns over has this program where you sort of adopt one of their residents, and give them a Christmas. They wouldn't get any presents otherwise. So I adopted Kiria."

"Do you know her?"

"No. And we won't meet. All I know is her first name, her age and size. And the shelter gave me this." She handed him a folded slip of paper from her knitting basket.

It was a wish list, written in round, girlish script: *A doll. A warm sweater. A pretty dress. A soccer ball. A diary.* His eyes fogged up. "Did you get her those things?" he asked.

"And more. Want to see?"

In a corner of the dining room there was a large picnic hamper. Annah lifted back the lid and took out the items one by one and laid them on the table, lovingly. She told him where she had bought each item, how she had chosen it. "The doll is the kind that is very popular with girls now."

He knew the twins had similar ones, but they were six. "I didn't know girls still played with dolls at nine."

"Kind of refreshing to find out they do, isn't it?" Annah smiled wistfully. "I wish I could have gotten all the dresses that went with her, but I kind of blew my budget on the doll herself."

"Then what are all these?" he asked, pointing to what looked like a rather extensive miniature wardrobe.

"Those I made," she said. "I hope she'll like them."

"*I* like them."

She laughed.

"No, really. I think what you're doing is wonderful."

"Don't give me too much credit, Luke. It's as much for me as it is for her. I love Christmas, and since I don't have any children of my own to—"

The tiny choking sound she made was his undoing. Was that longing he saw in her eyes? His gut gave him a vicious kick to get his attention. Then it made an excellent, albeit dangerous, point: *Who says a woman like her couldn't change her mind about having ba-*

bies? Once the thought was planted, it took root in Luke almost immediately. It was the only way he could marry Annah.

And that possibility was definitely intriguing—the possibility that Annah could be his bride.

Chapter Eight

Annah always held her big winter sale the day after Thanksgiving, so it was late when she finally closed up the secondhand shop Friday night. She was surprised to find Luke in the house.

"I thought you had a date tonight," she said.

"I canceled it."

"You're not feeling ill again, are you?" He looked fine, and he had told her that morning that he was back to one hundred percent, but she couldn't think of another reason why he'd cancel a date.

"I'm fine. I just wanted to spend tonight here. I want to talk with you."

It sounded like he needed her counsel. Well, she would do whatever she could. Finding out about his ex-fiancée had only made her more determined to help him.

After dinner they went into the living room, where the only light came from the fire Luke had built earlier. They sat on the two love seats, facing each other. Annah waited out the silence. He had said he wanted to talk to her, so she told herself that he would start when he was ready.

He started with a bang. "How do you know when a man and a woman are right for each other?" he asked.

Taken aback, she didn't reply. In order for him to be asking this, he must be getting close with one of the women. She wasn't expecting this, and not just because two nights earlier she had slept with him in his bed. Swallowing, she told herself to be happy for him. She wondered which one he had chosen, but he had never given her a hint before now.

He spoke again. "I mean the mysterious insight of yours that everybody in town talks about," he said, so seriously that she had to smile.

"Want to know something? It really isn't mysterious at all," she confessed. "Just finely tuned. Anyone who is open to recognizing true love can see it."

He seemed to be considering that. "I want to know if I'm seeing it, but I don't know where to start," he said. "What are the signs? What do I look for?"

She bit her lip, thinking. "It's not so much that you see it. It's more a feeling—a temperature, really. It's a warmth generated between two people." She paused, frowning. "Does this make sense?"

He was leaning forward, chin on hands, looking as if he were trying to understand someone speaking a foreign language, and not wanting to offend them. "Not really," he admitted at last.

She looked into the fire, trying to think of another way to explain it. A spark popped, giving her an inspiration. "Love is like a fire," she said.

He gave her a doubtful look.

"No, really!" she said. "Let me try to put it into

words. You know all about building a fire, Luke. First of all, you need that initial spark to get it going, right?''

"Yes," he said doubtfully. "But I don't see—"

"In love, that spark is attraction. And it keeps sparking even after the fire is going. You could call it the physical part of a relationship."

"I get it," he said, and from the look he gave her she knew he did. Most men "got" the physical part of it. That came naturally. Even more so for him, she suspected, after having shared a kiss with him. When she realized that she was staring at his lips, she quickly went on.

"When the fire is going, it settles into a steady burn," she said. "In love, that's what you would call compatibility."

"That's what I see between Erik and Julie? And between Whit and Drew?"

"You could say that. It's that part of love that makes you want to settle down together. If it's there, then the fire's built right, and it can heat a whole home. Everyone around the two people involved—especially their children, if they have any—basks in the glow of their commitment, their partnership, their mutual support and security. It's what I think of as the emotional part of love."

He moved over onto her love seat. "Annah, I've found that with—"

"I know compatibility is what you were looking for all along," she said, interrupting him, not ready to hear whom he had chosen. "But I'm not finished yet. There's another component to love, and it's the most important one of all. But it's also the hardest to find and to define."

"What is it?"

"It's the times when the fire burns hotter and brighter. The blaze of passion."

"I'm not sure I follow you. Isn't passion like the sparks?" he asked.

"It is, and it isn't. This is physical, but deeper. More profound. I think of it as spiritual. It's the most elusive aspect of love. Lots of people settle just for the first two, and never even know what they're missing." She took his hand and gazed at him earnestly. "I don't want you to do that, Luke. True love is a blend of all three, sometimes a spark, sometimes a steady warmth, sometimes a transcendent blaze. Do you understand now?"

He thought he did. He had felt that spark with Annah, all right. He knew physical attraction. That kiss they had shared had been popping with sparks, and that didn't count all the times he had resisted kissing her.

He'd found compatibility with Annah, too. Somehow their partnership had grown into friendship and beyond. He felt he could say anything to her. Why, just look at the conversation they were having! And it had been easy, living here with her, sharing her little dollhouse. Two fit as comfortably as one. They seemed to read each other's moods unerringly, knowing when to draw close, when to give space. When to reach out for support, when to give it. He hadn't ever known it before, but having experienced it, he was sure that that was compatibility.

But when she had talked about passion, that's when he knew that he understood exactly what she was saying. He had felt it two nights ago, a powerful sense of rightness, of blessedness, of his instincts crying out in joyous affirmation. If the time he had spent holding her in his arms hadn't been spiritual, then he didn't know what was. The feeling was starting to rise in him again, right now, with her hand in his.

But what if his feelings were steering him wrong again? This seemed like love to him, but he had to be certain. Then he remembered something she had said the other night, when she'd thought he was asleep. *Give your feelings another try. Trust in what they tell you. And when they tell you that you've found the one you truly love, trust that she'll love you, too... That's the way love works.*

"Annah," he began, hesitatingly. "True love is mutual, right?"

"By definition. If it isn't, then it's not really true love. It's someone trying to talk himself or herself into it." She gave his hand a gentle squeeze. "Like you said you did once."

Was he doing that again? He hoped not. But if he thought about it too much, his doubts started clamoring for attention. "How are you supposed to know for sure?" he asked.

"Just by trusting your feelings. Your heart won't steer you wrong, if you listen to it."

"Let me make sure I understand," he said. If he was going to go out on limb, he was going to edge his way out there, inch by inch. "Let's say I know this woman."

Her heart plummeted in her chest. She reminded herself that she was supposed to be helping him, so she concentrated on listening and not on the way it felt to have him so near, to look into his eyes, to feel her hand in his.

"Well, first off, let me say that there are plenty of sparks," he said. "Neither of us could deny that. Our physical attraction is mutual...and considerable."

Not wanting to think about him with another woman, Annah thought about the two of them instead. How her inner thermometer had been rising since the day she'd met him. About the shower of sparks their kiss had ignited. No doubt about it, she and Luke had physical attraction to burn.

He went on. "And we've had plenty of time to find out that we're compatible. We've spent a lot of time together and I know she finds it as easy to be with me as I do to be with her. Sometimes I get this eerie feeling that she knows what I'm thinking, and sometimes I think I know her thoughts, too."

Annah remembered the knowing way he always looked at her, his penetrating glances. She wondered if he knew what she was thinking right now, too.

"We've been partners from the word go, and her house is the only place in the world I've ever felt at home. That's compatibility, right? The emotional part you were talking about."

He was looking at her, his eyes never wavering. Then it hit her. Dear God, was he talking about her? Them?

"Isn't it, Annah?" he asked again, softly.

Wordlessly she nodded. Still holding her hand in his, he slid closer and put his other arm around her.

"The third part is tricky, you said. It's passion, but in a broad sense. It's deep. It's profound. It's spiritual." He paused and lowered his voice to a whisper. "I know what you mean, because I think…I think I've felt that, too."

He swallowed. "But I don't know if she has. She has to feel it too, doesn't she? Because if it's not mutual…"

Then it's not true love. They each finished the

thought in their head, neither wanting to speak it aloud. The silence opened like a chasm between them. When it became more than she could bear, he said, ''I have to find out. And forgive me, but I can only think of one way to do that.''

Slowly he lowered his mouth to hers. Tenderly he touched her lips. His kiss was soft, chaste, reverent. But it was powerful. It tapped into a well of feelings inside her, feelings that warmed and spread and overflowed. They filled places in her that had been empty for a long time and places that had always been empty.

He felt her lips go soft and pliant under his. It felt so good, so right, but it wasn't enough. He had to know if she felt it, too. Keeping their mouths joined, he eased back until he was lying on the small couch with her on top of him. With their bodies sealed together, touching from lips to toes, a song of completeness was begun. And having her on top meant that she could choose to continue the contact or break it off.

She kept the kiss going. He was under her now, solid and real, a prince and a man and a dream come true. She felt the strength of him, the heat, and it didn't end at his body but washed over into hers. This wasn't sexual, but something more profound. She was caught up in a magnetic force field, but felt empowered, not trapped, by it. With this positive energy around her, within her, there was nothing she could not do. What was it? It was too vast to put a name to, too potent to define. All she knew was that she had never felt this way before, an inferno ignited within her.

Glowing from her response, a response he could feel as strongly as his own, his intuition started talking to him again. At first he was too caught up in the kiss to listen, but it threaded its way through into his consciousness.

She does! it said.

She does what? Luke wondered to himself.

She does feel it, too. Can't you tell?

And he could tell. Overwhelmed by the knowledge, he released her mouth and put his lips to her ear. "Annah, I think I've found out what I wanted to know," he murmured.

The vibration of his voice against her ear was a sensual distraction from his words. What had he wanted to know? She couldn't remember and didn't want to have to stop feeling in order to think.

"You do feel it, too, don't you?" he asked.

Unease began to condense in Annah. She had told him how to recognize true love, and now he thought he had found it in her. But it couldn't be!

Rationality returned with a rush, reminding her that the flame she had felt from the beginning was just empathy, the sparks just physical desire. True, they were compatible in most ways, but that wasn't enough. And what she had been feeling right now…that was—no. She had to remind herself how fire held the power of light and heat but also of destruction. She had to put out this blaze, now, before it destroyed them both. Because if he thought she was his true love, he would want her for his bride. And that she could not be.

She pushed away from him and got to her feet— quickly, before she could change her mind. "Luke, no. It's not what you think."

He stood next to her, a troubled frown spreading over his face. "You told me not to think. You told me to feel."

"Yes, but don't feel it for me! Luke, whatever is

between us is…it just can't be right. I've told you from the beginning that I'm not what you're looking for in a wife."

"Yes, but you never told me why. Not in so many words." After all this, he felt he had a right to know. If babies weren't her thing, there had to be a reason. And if he knew the reason, he had a chance of changing her mind.

"You want to know why?" she said, her voice rising with emotion. "Fine. I'll spell it out for you, loud and clear. You want to have children, and I'm not having any! Period. End of discussion."

She turned and stormed out of the room. In the wake of her sudden outburst, he stood unmoving, conscious only of the fact that once again his feelings had done him wrong. And that this time it hurt even more.

Annah went upstairs shaking with the effort of holding back her tears. How had things turned into such a mess? All she had wanted was to help Luke find what she couldn't—the happiness of true love and a family. And now look what had happened. She had finally gotten him to listen to his feelings, and then she'd had to tell him they were wrong! She had hated hurting him, but she had no choice but to be direct. It was the only way to make sure he would forget this whole thing with her and turn his attention to someone else before it was too late. She would still help him in whatever way she could, even though the thought of him with another woman, no matter how deserving, cut like a dull, rusty blade.

Of course she couldn't sleep. After a while she heard Luke come upstairs, get ready for bed, go to bed. Long after there was silence in his room she continued to toss and turn restlessly, spinning useless matchmaking plans and holding her tears in, aching and silent.

Halfway through the night she crumbled, after a trip to the bathroom for aspirin and a hot water bottle. Tonight, this was the last straw. Even now, long after her marriage had ended, this physical pain only added to her emotional pain, month after month. There was no reason for her to be pregnant now, but still her womb gathered itself to weep for the baby that would not be. And Annah wept with it.

Luke lay awake, staring at the ceiling, trying in vain to make sense of something that was completely incomprehensible to him. How could something feel so right and be so wrong? But it must be. *He* must be wrong. After all, he had done this before; he was a seasoned veteran at making a fool of himself over a woman. Annah, on the other hand, knew what she was talking about; at least he could have faith in that. Everyone knew that she was the expert when it came to love. And this wasn't it, according to her.

In the darkness he grimaced. Apparently he had let his physical desire take precedence again, as it had the time he had nearly married the wrong woman. But no matter how many ways he looked at it, it was different with Annah! He desired her, certainly. But it hadn't hit him so hard before. And that wasn't all. There was that feeling of ease, that comfort, the friendship that spoke of compatibility. He certainly hadn't felt that before, either. And he didn't even feel it with the women he was dating here at the Point, the ones with whom he was supposed to be so damn compatible. They might match up on paper, but Annah was the one he was drawn to for conversation, for support, for companion-ship.

And what about that other, more profound feeling he had gotten with her? Had he just imagined that, as she had said, because he wanted to make it all fit?

No, he just didn't buy that. He hadn't even heard of such a thing until she had explained it to him tonight, in front of the fire. What's more, he hadn't been look-ing for love, much less with Annah of all people, be-cause from the beginning she had made it clear that she was unsuitable as a bride for him. She still was. And that was another thing that made Annah different. Unlike his ex-fiancée, she had always been up-front about not wanting kids, even though she knew his true identity as a prince. If he didn't know better, he would almost think that she was protecting him from her.

His mind churned it all over for hours, until a sound from down the hall cut in on his thoughts. The re-mainder of the night he spent listening to Annah's heart pour out its grief and fighting his inexplicable desire to give comfort to the woman who had spurned him. Afraid that even if he had so little pride as to offer it, his attempt would be an unwelcome intrusion on her pain.

What was fueling her anguish? It was heartrending, to lie there and listen. He knew it had to have some-thing to do with what had happened that night. But if she didn't feel the way he did, why would her feelings be so intense? They were, though. She had been dis-tressed from the time he had suggested that she shared his feelings. It had almost been like she had gotten defensive when she'd told him she wasn't what he was looking for in a wife. Something had struck a nerve, or she wouldn't have gotten so upset. And she had certainly been that when she'd told him she wasn't having children.

Then he realized something else. He had asked her point-blank, but she still hadn't told him *why*. And because of that, this wasn't over yet. Not as far as he was concerned. Asking her directly hadn't worked, but he might learn something by observation. If he couldn't rely on his feelings, he would settle for some cold, hard facts.

The sound of Annah's alarm didn't waken Luke the next morning, because he had never gone to sleep. But when the alarm continued to sound after a few minutes, concern for her took him to her room. She was all right—just sound asleep, buried under a mountain of covers. Frowning, he turned off the alarm. He had never known her to do this. Usually she woke and turned off the alarm before it ever rang.

His eyes swept the room, stopping at the sight of a hot water bottle that had fallen to the floor beside her bed. He picked it up and turned it over in his hands, thinking, then set it on the nightstand. Still she slept. He figured she needed it, after the night she'd had. So he backed silently out of her room.

Wilfred was the first one in the coffee shop as usual, Eldridge shadowing him. They took their accustomed seats.

But Luke wasn't at his. He was behind the counter. "Morning," he greeted them.

They stared at him. "What the hell are you doing back there?" Wilfred asked.

"We want Annah," Eldridge chimed in.

"Well, you've got me. She's a little under the

weather this morning,'' Luke said. ''What can I get for you?''

''Annah's never sick,'' Wilfred declared.

''Maybe she's got that influenza that's been goin' around,'' Eldridge mused.

''Must've caught it from him,'' Wilfred said accusingly, pointing a gnarled finger Luke's way.

''Fine way to pay her back for nursing him while he was sick.''

Luke stood his ground behind the counter. ''It's not the flu,'' he told them. ''She's just been working too hard lately. So I'm taking over this morning.''

''You?''

''Ha!''

He gave them a look he usually reserved for cabinet members who needed a reminder that their job, like his, was to *serve* their country. ''Gentlemen, if you're not going to order anything, leave those stools for some paying customers.''

Wilfred looked at him consideringly. ''Coffee, black,'' he said after a moment.

''Coffee, regular,'' said Eldridge.

Luke poured two coffees and set them down, putting the cream and sugar in front of Eldridge.

Wilfred took a long slurp of coffee, then set his cup back down. ''What'd ya make for pastries, hotshot?'' he asked.

Luke jerked a thumb over his shoulder. ''Got some day-old muffins,'' he said. Annah had extras left from yesterday—business had been slow, the day after a holiday. ''Take them or leave them.''

''I'll take one. Blueberry.''

''Bran.''

When the muffins had been reduced to scattered

crumbs, Luke took their plates away and poured them each a refill. Wilfred was reading the newspaper. "Big spread here in the *Gazette* 'bout Jimmy Turner," he said to Luke.

"Who's that?" Luke asked. He'd never heard the name before.

"Who's that?" Eldridge echoed. "The man Annah was married to, that's who's that."

Luke wasn't expecting that. He didn't know her ex was still around.

"Local boy makes good," Wilfred went on. "Jimmy was born and raised here on the Point."

"Not Annah. Brought her home from that fancy college he went to in Illinois," Eldridge offered.

"Indiana."

"Wherever."

"Course, Jimmy moved away, after they got divorced."

"Ayup," said Eldridge in agreement. "He's long gone now."

"Went way up to Nogglenotch," Wilfred said.

"Must be four, five miles from here," Eldridge added gravely. "Maybe five and a quarter."

Despite himself, Luke smiled. "How did he get in the *Gazette?*" he asked, trying not to show his curiosity. It was a natural question.

"Started himself up one of them computer software businesses," Wilfred said.

"High-tech," added Eldridge.

"On-line."

"Ayup, he's a real mover and a shaker, Jimmy is. Hear he works all hours."

"Says here he's the biggest employer in the town."

"Got himself a…"

The conversation went on, but Luke didn't hear the rest. More customers started coming in, and he got real busy real fast. Things didn't go quite as smoothly as when Annah was there—he had forgotten about getting water ready for the tea drinkers, and he broke two glasses. But when he told people he was filling in because Annah needed a break, they were all very understanding. Even Mrs. Cartelli, on whom he spilled orange juice, didn't make one teasing remark. It was like they were pulling together for his sake as well as for Annah's.

He felt like an insider. And besides that, he just might have inadvertently gotten a clue as to why Annah was crying last night.

A ray of sunlight shining right on her face woke Annah up. Why didn't she sleep with the shade pulled down, so this wouldn't happen? she wondered sleepily. Then it struck her that this had never happened before. Why not?

She sat bolt upright in bed. Because ever since she had opened the coffee shop, she had been awake before dawn, every day except major holidays. And this was no holiday. She had overslept! She looked at the clock and groaned. Her customers! They would either be lined up at the door in the cold, or worse, long gone by now.

Checking her alarm, she saw that it had been turned off. She must have done it in her sleep. Jumping out of bed, she made a mental note to move her clock to her dresser across the room, so she'd have to get out of bed to turn off her alarm. Then this wouldn't happen again.

Throwing on clothes, she chastised herself. *No won-*

der things like this happen, when you stay up all night bawling your eyes out, girl! It's all your own fault.

And Luke's, she reminded herself, overtaken by a sudden burst of anger. He had no right to come here and start stirring things up in her life. Those things were better left where they were, abandoned and forgotten. And now he had this idea that he loved her! Men! she fumed, dragging a brush through her hair. Couldn't any one of them tell the difference between love and lust?

She was in and out of the bathroom in record time and flew down the stairs. She was in no danger of thinking she was in love with Luke, she told herself, as long as she kept reminding herself what he really wanted. And there was no way she was setting herself up for that again. Luke was no different from Jimmy. And Jimmy—

She stood in the doorway to the coffee shop, stopped dead in her tracks by what she saw. It was open. It was functional. It looked like every other morning…except different. As customers got up to leave, they brought their dirty dishes over to the counter. They were leaving their money there, too, without having been rung up. Where were they getting the coffee? she wondered.

And then she saw Luke, behind the counter, making a fresh pot. He didn't see her standing there at the inner door. She watched him in wonder as he took care of the dirty dishes, then wiped off the counter, which already looked spotless. Then he took an order from some new arrivals who sat there. Annah leaned against the doorjamb, speechless. He was born royalty—a prince, a ruler of a small but wealthy land—and here he was waiting on common people in her little shop. Why?

It was obvious. He had done it for her. Now Annah knew how her alarm had gotten turned off, and the sweetness of that small gesture as much as the big effort she saw before her brought a lump of tears to her throat. Luke filled a tray and carried it over to one of the booths, and on the way back he finally saw her. His immediate reaction was a warm smile, and she felt the lump in her throat grow.

"Feeling better?" he asked.

She was feeling worse, oh, so much worse. She could no longer pretend he was just like Jimmy, who would have been too wrapped up in his own concerns to ever notice hers. "How...how did you do all this?" she asked.

"You do it all," he reminded her, moving back behind the counter again. But he sounded proud of himself, and with good reason.

She almost joined him automatically, then saw that his seat at the counter was empty. She sat down in it. "Yes, but I know how. I've been doing it awhile."

He put a cup of tea in front of her, her favorite kind. "Well, I've been watching you awhile," he said, so low that only she could hear.

She took a sip of her tea, remembering that first afternoon, when he didn't even know how to make a cup of tea. "It wasn't too long ago that you couldn't have done this," she said.

"You've taught me a few things, Annah. And I'm figuring out the rest for myself," he said, and the look he sent her told her he wasn't just talking about making tea.

She purposely ignored the double entendre. "Yes, this place is really up and running. Thanks, Luke. You saved me."

"Well, your customers were a big help. They're bringing up their dishes and paying what they owe. I didn't have time to figure out how to unlock the cash register. And they're eating yesterday's muffins without a complaint."

"There are enough of them?"

"Well, I realized after a while that it was going to be close. So they've been settling for 'halvsies.'"

"You learned that from the twins, didn't you?"

"Ayup," he said with a grin, and left her to wait on one of the tables. Annah watched him, warmth welling up inside of her. She could tell herself that it was from drinking hot tea, she could tell herself it was from knowing that her business was under control, she could tell herself it was because she was happy that, thanks in part to her, he was going to make some other woman a great husband.

But she was having a hard time believing herself.

Chapter Nine

Luke flew around the perimeter of the rink, taking a warm-up skate before the Wednesday night hockey game started. It was four days since he had manned the coffee shop for Annah—four days closer to the Firehouse Dance and his self-imposed engagement deadline. Four days closer to his marriage deadline. He should have been feeling increased pressure, but what he was feeling was increased clarity.

The goalie for his team came out of the chute from the locker room without looking, right into his path. Luke pulled up abruptly, his blade sending up an arcing shower of ice chips. The goalie gave a low whistle to show he was impressed. Luke grinned and gave him a tap on the shin pads with his stick. "Brick wall tonight, buddy," he said.

"Got one in front of me," his teammate replied, skating toward the net.

Luke resumed his warm-up and his thoughts. He was feeling strong and confident. He hadn't frittered away the past four days, even though he hadn't been on one date. He had spent his time watching Annah, and thinking.

Being on her side of the counter on Saturday morning, waiting on her customers, had brought him a staggering realization. Annah was successful, but she was no businesswoman at heart. She was a nurturer. Just look at the businesses she had chosen—feeding and clothing people! He would bet a large portion of the palace treasury that she had taken her divorce settlement and gone into business not by choice, but by default. Because she didn't have a family to nurture.

It all made sense. A woman like Annah was a natural to be a mother. And why wasn't she? He owed that bit of illumination to Wilfred and Eldridge. If her ex-husband was a mover and shaker, no doubt he had been more focused on having the business he wanted than on having the kids Annah wanted. Jerk.

Luke moved in line for a passing drill. He could see now that the busyness of her life was a way for her to fill up its emptiness. The puck sailed his way, and he handled it and sent it down the line. She seemed calm and in control, but she wasn't really at peace. His guess was that after her marriage had blown up, she had given up and resigned herself to a life alone.

Babies aren't my thing. The hell they weren't! Over the past weeks he had seen her play with toddlers whose moms were busy trying on clothes, wipe dribbly chins whose owners sat in high chairs in the coffee shop, secretly slip tiny sweaters she had hand knit onto the shelves of her secondhand store and give a trembling sigh as she watched them leave the shop worn by wiggly little bundles carried out in their mommies' arms.

But the life she had resigned herself to wasn't working, and if she couldn't see that, he sure could. His job was to get her to see that deep down she did still want kids—his kids. If ol' Jimmy hadn't wanted to give them to her, that was past history. Luke was ready, willing and able to be of service. The fact that she was edgy around him—more than a little—he took as a good sign. She might think she had been able to forget that kiss, or the night she had spent in his bed, or the evening in front of the fire, but he had a feeling it was all still there inside her, burning too hot to ignore. Hell, he was burning up himself. He didn't know how she was handling it, but for him, being here on the ice tonight would help take the edge off.

He skated over to the bench, where the captain was starting to give the lineup. They were playing another team from the Point, so the other players looked familiar to Luke. All except the goalie, who was turning back every shot his teammates sent his way during warm-ups.

"Who's that, Carl?" Luke asked. "Never saw him before."

The captain looked up from his clipboard. "That's because he moved away a few years ago. He's got a business, so he's too busy to play regularly, but he fills in for them when they need him. Name's Turner."

Luke played a hunch. "Jimmy Turner?" he asked.

Carl gave him a direct stare. "That's right," he said.

"Do me a favor, buddy," Luke said. "Put me in your spot tonight." It was petty. It was pointless. It was macho. But a petty, pointless, macho act of revenge would be a good outlet for some of the frustration that was boiling up inside him.

"You play center?" Carl asked.

Luke understood the question. He had been playing defense to fill in for one of the guys who had been injured when he joined the team. But it was hard not to smile. He had grown up on the Constellation Isles. He'd been skating since he could walk. Center had been his position all through school. Asking if he could play it was like asking if he could breathe.

"Been known to," was all he said in reply.

"All right, Hansson. Center for the second line. Let's see what you've got."

Turner was good. A real competitor. He seemed to know Luke was gunning for him and to enjoy it. But midway through the second period Luke got off a good slapshot. *Take that, you bastard,* he thought as the puck left his stick. The shot hit the goalie's chest with such force that it knocked him into the net. By the end of the game Luke had scored two more goals, another screaming slapshot and a pretty little wrister that finessed the pads off the guy. The first two were for him, but that last one was purely for Annah.

He skated over and shook hands with Jimmy Turner at the end of the game. "Nice hat trick," the goalie acknowledged.

"Good game," Luke returned.

But the game was over, and it was time to get serious. On the ice he had avenged his woman. But in real life he still had to win her.

Saturday afternoon was especially busy in Annah's shop, because everyone who hadn't done so already came in to buy a dress for the next weekend's dance. When the last customer left, she leaned against the door with a weary sigh. The week had gone by so quickly,

between working and coordinating plans for the refreshments, that she had barely had time to think.

And not thinking had left room for insight. Talking
with Luke about love in front of the fire was supposed
to have been for his benefit. She was his matchmaker,
sharing her wisdom, what she had learned, to help him.
But teaching him had thrown light on some of the dark
recesses of her past. All week the illumination had increased. And now she knew.

It was a startling realization, finding out that she had
gotten married for the wrong reason. Now she could
see her mistake, but then she had been young—just out
of college—and she'd had her heart set on starting a
family right away. It was so clear now that what she
had thought was true love was merely compatibility,
so clear why things had turned out the way they had.
No babies, no marriage—no wonder. Her marriage
hadn't failed for lack of children, but for lack of love.

And now here was Luke, and all the things he was
making her feel. She had tried to steer clear of him all
week, and he had kept a respectful—but watchful—
distance. She wondered if he still thought she could be
the bride he was looking for. And why shouldn't he?
Even to her, it seemed they had it all, and that was
scary. But no doubt she was just conjuring up those
feelings of true love, because she so badly wanted it to
be. Real as they seemed, she couldn't give in to them.
She couldn't give him false hope. Because she wasn't
the right woman for him. Not because he was a prince,
and had an obligation to his country to produce heirs.
But because he was a man, and had a dream of being
a father. She couldn't stand in the way of Luke's having his dream come true.

"Hi."

His single syllable broke into her reverie. The sight of him there inside the doorway made her heart bounce. "Hi," she answered.

He looked around and gave a low whistle. "Wow. I've never seen this place so torn apart."

"It was so busy I couldn't keep up with putting things away."

He began straightening up the shelves, as naturally as if he had been doing such menial tasks all his royal life. Joining in, she started tackling the dressing room. They worked in a silence that would have been compatible a few weeks ago. Now there was an edge to it that Annah preferred to ignore rather than explore.

She snapped out of her thoughts when he spoke. "How are things going for the Firehouse Dance?" he asked.

She had a feeling there was more than idle conversation behind his question, but she answered conversationally. "The planning, assigning and buying are finished. This week I'll be devoting all my time to baking. As far as I know, the work of the other committees is progressing well." She paused, then let curiosity get the better of her. "Who will you be taking, Luke?" she asked.

"No one. But I know who I want to take." *You,* he thought, and told her so with a look. But her gaze skittered away, and he knew that she was shutting him out. Her words confirmed it.

"Then you should ask her," she said, purposely misunderstanding.

The frustration that had been building in him all week rose like the tide coming in. She wasn't even going to give him a chance. "I made it clear to the women I'm dating that I'll be there alone," he said shortly.

She looked concerned. "Are you sure that's such a good strategy?"

"It's not strategy at all. It's just a survival tactic. I'm going to propose to the woman I'm going to spend the rest of my life with that night, remember?" One of the women he was "just friends" with. One of the women he still gave no more than a chaste good-night kiss, the kind you gave the wife of a friend.

"I know," she said softly.

"Given that I haven't made a choice yet, I figure that by going stag, at least I'll have the flexibility to choose right there. What else am I supposed to do?" he asked irritably. "Promise to escort one woman to the dance and maybe end the night with another as my fiancée? I'm afraid my strong grounding in protocol simply wouldn't allow that. It would be in very bad form."

"You don't have to be sarcastic."

And you don't have to be so stubborn, he wanted to say, but bit down on the urge. "We princes are like that. Not so charming as people think, when our backs are against the wall. You of all people ought to know what it's like to feel pushed like that. Have any of the town busybodies prevailed upon you to accept an escort for the dance yet?"

"No. I'll be there alone."

He wasn't surprised that Annah had resisted all fix-ups, as she had said she would. Stubborn, through and through. If she said babies weren't her thing, she'd stick to it to the grave and beyond. Dammit, he needed a way to budge her.

Suddenly, he thought of one. "Good," he said

briskly. "Because I'll require your services that evening."

"What for?"

"What else? Matchmaking."

Busy as she herself was, Annah knew exactly what Luke did that week—whom he went out with, where they went. He seemed to be redoubling his efforts, because he saw each of the women twice. *Good!* the matchmaker in her applauded. *That's just what he should be doing.* But the woman in her suffered silently, wishing for things she had no right to wish for.

Her secondhand shop was closed on Saturday afternoon, so that she could get the refreshments ready for the dance that night. When the last box was packed, Luke appeared, to help her take them over to the firehouse. They made several trips, and then Annah stayed to finish setting things up with the rest of the committee. It was getting late, so they agreed Luke should go home and take the first shift in the bathroom.

When he had finished showering, he heard a knock at the door to the secondhand shop. Throwing on jeans and a sweater, he went downstairs and opened it to an attractive, blond woman he hadn't seen before.

"I know you're closed," she said, "but I'm desperate. I need a dress for the dance and it's too late to drive all the way to the mall."

Luke knew Annah would never turn away a desperate woman, so he stepped aside and let her in. "Why did you leave it until the last minute?" he asked, turning up the lights.

"I didn't," she said. "I got a dress last month, but I just went to put it on and it doesn't fit." He must have looked blank, because she added, "I'm pregnant, and I didn't think I'd be showing this soon."

He steered her over to the maternity dresses. "This your first one?"

She smiled. "No. I've got a preschooler and a toddler at home playing with their daddy," she said, sifting through the rack. "My husband has always dreamed of having enough kids for a basketball team."

"Looks like you're about halfway there."

She took a few choices into the dressing room. "Are you sure Annah won't mind?"

"I'm sure," Luke told her, thinking that this woman must not know Annah at all, to ask that.

Annah came home just as Luke was ringing up the sale. She seemed taken aback when she looked at the woman.

"Last-minute sale, for the dance," Luke explained as he handed the woman her change. "Maternity."

Annah looked at the woman. "Congratulations, Ellen," she said. The untrained ear wouldn't have picked anything up, but she sounded strangely quiet to Luke. He knew her so well now that he seemed keyed in to all the nuances of her feelings.

"Thanks," the woman said, and then looked at Luke. "And thank you," she said, holding up the dress. "I don't know what I would have done otherwise."

"You're welcome," Luke said. "See you at the dance."

"Yes, I suppose I will. Goodbye, Annah."

"Goodbye."

Annah stood looking at the door after it had closed. She looked shaken. "Annah, what's the matter?" Luke asked, concerned.

She shook her head and turned away. "Nothing," she said.

He knew her better than that. "Annah, why—" he began, approaching her.

"It's nothing, Luke. Really," she said, facing him, a big fake smile plastered across her face.

"Annah, who—"

But before he could finish, she interrupted him again. "Gosh, it's getting late! I'd better go upstairs and get ready," she said, leaving him alone with his unanswered questions. All of them.

Annah stood before her mirror, absently putting the finishing touches on her hair. Her reflected image looked good, she thought, in the detached way of a professional in the business evaluating a piece of merchandise. She had set aside the dress a few months ago, when it had first come into the shop. It was a shimmering topaz that complemented her brown hair and eyes. Its uneven hemline was designed to draw attention to the legs, not that hers would be visible behind the refreshment table.

Wasn't the fair maiden supposed to be excited, when she was dressing to go to a ball with the prince? It was funny, how her life had gone. It was Cinderella's story turned upside down. For weeks she had been living her dream come true with her prince. But after the ball, the dream would be shattered. He would marry someone else, and she would be left alone with her unfulfilled longings.

She couldn't change the way the story ended, but she could play her part as best she could. So she put down her brush, put on a brave face and went downstairs to the waiting prince.

Luke turned from the window when he heard Annah coming down the stairs. The sight of her nearly took his breath away. Her dress glistened with gold in the soft light, clinging mysteriously to her curves, swaying with each graceful step. He had never seen a woman who was more like a princess, in looks and carriage. If only she would be one in name, as well. His name.

He walked up next to her, and the princess was a woman, the woman whose dark eyes captivated him. "You are beautiful," he said simply, because it was the truest way he could express what was in his heart. She didn't just look beautiful, she was beautiful, inside and out.

If her lips started to tremble, she covered it up by giving him a wide smile. "You don't look so bad yourself," she said lightly. "For an ordinary guy."

In fact, he looked like a prince again, in the charcoal suit he'd been wearing on the day he had shown up on her doorstep. She remembered her powerful reaction to him, and realized that time had only strengthened it. Standing this close to him, it took a physical and mental effort to keep her feelings hidden.

The phone rang. He took the call, and it was for him. "Thanks for letting me know," he said. "But you won't have to hold them off much longer for me."

He had told Annah that one of his cabinet ministers was keeping the council of elders apprised of his progress.

"Yes. Tonight." He was looking at Annah now. "One way or another. I'll call you with a name tomorrow morning."

He hung up the phone, still watching her. "Are you sure you're ready to go?"

"Yes, I think so," she said. "All the refreshments are there, and—"

"What I mean is, was there anything else you wanted to do...or say...before we leave?"

He was giving her a deep look that she couldn't quite meet. "No. Nothing at all," she said, reaching for her wrap.

He looked at her for a moment more before saying briskly, "Then let's get this show on the road."

He insisted on driving her to the dance. It wasn't far, but it would be long enough for his purpose of getting her undivided attention.

"This is not a good idea," she warned. "People are going to think we're going to the dance together."

"We are going to the dance together," he pointed out.

"You know what I mean. *Together* together. I don't want to scare any of your eligible women off." Actually, Annah hadn't wanted to be alone with Luke like this. The intimacy of being with him now, enclosed together in the small space inside his sports car, made what she would be losing that night all the more poignant.

"Oh, I think these Down East women are made of sterner stuff than that," he said, negotiating a curve in the road.

"How can you be so calm? You're going to get engaged tonight, and you don't even know to whom!"

He shrugged. "I guess it's because I trust you, Annah."

"Me? What do you mean?"

"I'm talking about your helping me tonight, of course."

As he had expected, she balked at that. "But, Luke, it's out of my hands now," she said. "There's no one new to introduce you to at the dance. I've done my part as a matchmaker. You have four excellent candidates who meet your requirements."

"I know," he said calmly. "The problem is, I can't seem to choose one of the four. That's why I need your help."

"No you don't. You're just getting cold feet. It's perfectly understandable," she said, sounding like she was rationalizing, which she was. "Go with your feelings, Luke."

"The last time I tried to do that, I seem to recall your telling me that my feelings were wrong," he said, giving her a pointed look.

She gulped and said nothing.

"I have too much at stake to risk being wrong."

"Then go with your intellect! Go with anything! Just choose one."

"All right," he said amiably. "I'll choose the woman you tell me is my true love."

Her mouth dropped open. "You want me to—no way! I couldn't possibly—"

"Don't be modest, Annah. You're a legend around here, you and that mysterious insight of yours. I'm asking you to use it for me."

"You want me to pick a *bride* for you?"

"In a manner of speaking. I can't think of a better way to do it, myself."

She shook her head. "This is too much to ask of me," she declared.

That, he thought, was exactly the point. If she felt about him the way he hoped she did, it would be pure hell for her to choose a wife for him. "Is it?" he asked, pulling the car into a parking space. "When I came here, you agreed to help me, remember?"

"But that was before—" She stopped, staring at him.

He turned and looked right at her, so close in the confines of the small car. "Before what, Annah?" he asked, his voice low and intense. "Before we started living together? Before we kissed? Before we—"

"That has nothing to do with this, and you know it!"

"Do I? You're the expert on love, but it seems to me that those are things that shouldn't be ignored."

Didn't he get it? They *had* to ignore those things! "Luke, don't do this," she warned him. "This is your future, your life. I can't make this decision for you. It's too much responsibility."

He knew that. But if she was going to turn her back on what it seemed to him they had—if she was going to turn her back on *him,* so that he had no choice but to marry someone else—then she was going to have to take responsibility for it herself.

"Luke, it should be *your* choice."

"It is," he said. "And I choose you to make it. If I can't trust my feelings on this, Annah, I will have to trust yours." He lowered his voice to a whisper. "Don't let me down."

Annah stood behind the refreshment table in an agony of indecision. Luke wasn't kidding. He really wanted her to use her insight to find his true love. In a bid to buy some time, she had told him to dance with all of the candidates. He had taken her advice without question, moving with ease within the crowds in the hall, talking to almost everyone he passed. Again, Annah had to remind herself that he was a prince, he seemed so at home here in a small-town firehouse decorated with ribbons, balloons and bunting.

He found Terri first, and was on the floor with her now. She looked like she was enjoying herself immensely. Terri always did. She had a gift for seeing the humor in life and making a present of it for those around her as well as for herself. A little needle of pain pierced Annah's heart as she realized Terri would make him a fine princess.

So would Marilyn, whom he chose for his next partner. She already had the twins and was a terrific mother. Their marriage would make Luke an instant father, and while he still would want kids of his own, he would love Jenny and Janine dearly. Swift and sharp, a second needle found a home next to the first.

There was a rush of customers at the refreshment table. Annah served up punch and cookies automatically, too wrapped up in what was happening on the other side of the dance floor to take much notice in what was happening right under her nose. When the crowd subsided, she saw Luke dancing with Carol, and another needle hit the mark. Carol loved adventure—and she would take on the role of his princess with the same joy she found in the challenge of mountain climbing or white-water rafting.

Annah looked away, trying in vain to ease the stinging pain inside her. And then a final needle struck her when she looked back and saw Luke with Joyce this time. Joyce was absolutely unflappable. She could handle the stress of life in the public eye with grace and aplomb. And, of course, Joyce had an affinity for little kids.

Annah turned away. This was impossible! How was

she supposed to pick one of these women? How could they all seem so…okay? She tried to use her gift, but she didn't see true love between Luke and any of them. Maybe she had lost her insight, or more likely her pain had clouded it. Either way, she would have to find Luke and tell him she couldn't pick, because her insight was gone.

All of a sudden the air around her got ten degrees warmer. She didn't have to turn around to know that Luke was standing behind her. Without a word he put an arm around her waist and led her out from behind the table. Was it her imagination, or did the crowd begin to buzz as they walked onto the dance floor?

"What are you doing?" she asked, holding herself stiff as he pulled her into his arms.

"Dancing," he replied. "Although if you have to ask, I suppose I'm not doing a very good job of it."

He was, in fact, doing an excellent job of it. No one in Anders Point danced like this. No wonder the women he had danced with before looked like they were swooning in his arms. Annah felt that could be a distinct possibility, if she didn't stay on her guard. "It just seems different, without a dust rag in my hand, Your Highness," she said dryly.

"Stop playing Cinderella," he told her. "If I hadn't brought you out here you would have stayed behind that refreshment table all night."

"I have a job to do."

"Yes, you do. You're working for me now, Annah," he growled. "I know you've been watching me all night. Now tell me what you're feeling."

Did he really think she could put that into words? she wondered. As his arms closed more tightly around her, her last resistance went up in smoke, and she let herself melt against him. It felt so good. More, it felt so *right*. She buried her face against his shoulder, blocking out the sights and sounds, shutting out the knowledge that this was wrong. Just for a moment she let herself pretend that she wasn't handing him over to another woman tonight, that they would leave the dance together, and he would propose to her, Annah Lane. And that she would say yes, and they would get married and live happily ever after.

And in that moment the truth that she'd been blocking from her mind with all of her strength came rushing in on her like water over a burst dam. Her true-love insight wasn't gone. It just had never hit her so squarely in the heart before.

She was his true love.

The realization flooded through her, strong and vibrant and pulsing with life and rightness. She clung to him tighter, just to steady herself against the onslaught, and felt his arms close about her protectively. No wonder it had been so hard—impossible, in fact—to choose between the other women. She couldn't pick someone else for him—because she was his true love.

"Is everything all right?" he asked, his voice husky with tenderness. The sound of it made her ache with unexpressed feelings for him. But those had to stay safely behind the dam, even in the wake of her realization. Everything, in fact, was all wrong.

She loved him so much that she had to choose not to love him. Because true love or not, she just wasn't the kind of woman he wanted—needed—to marry.

"Fine," she choked out. She opened her eyes again, purposely letting in the harsh light of reality. In various places around the room she saw the four women he had been dating. Every one of them wanted babies.

Every one would be a wonderful mother. And one of them would share her life with the man Annah loved.

"Have you figured it out yet, Annah?" he asked softly. "Are you ready to tell me which woman in the room I should take to be my wife?"

There was no point in prolonging this. Any one of them would do—any one but her. She stepped back from his arms, shaking with tension. "I won't answer that," she told him quietly. "You came to me for help, and I gave you what you wanted. They're all compatible. They'll all be good mothers. Pick one, Luke, and...and best...best wi—"

She couldn't finish. With a choking noise she turned and fled, threading her way through the crowd and out of the swinging double doors that led to the kitchen.

Chapter Ten

Luke spun on his heels, but ran smack into something. Someone, actually. Someone who was almost as tall as he was and just as solid.

It was Jimmy Turner.

"What did you do to her, Hansson?" he asked softly, but Luke could hear the undertone of menace in his voice.

"None of your business, you—"

Suddenly a third voice broke in. A woman's. "Come on, honey. Let it go. She probably just had to go into the kitchen to check on the refreshments. Anyway, it's between them."

The woman hanging on Jimmy's arm looked at Luke apologetically. "He's a little overprotective," she said. "You see, no one's really gotten involved with Annah since the divorce, and he just doesn't want to see her get hurt."

Luke stared at her. *Jimmy* didn't want to see Annah get hurt! But he was the one who had hurt her! Then he looked at the woman again. It was the blonde who had been in the shop earlier. The one who was pregnant for the third time.

The one whose husband had always wanted enough kids for a basketball team.

Before Luke could process this new information, there was a big commotion at the front door. He swung around and saw two men with cameras pushing their way into the room. "There he is!" one shouted, pointing right at Luke.

Luke felt like he had taken a hit. Damn! The paparazzi had finally gotten on his trail, and their timing couldn't be worse. He knew his identity would have been revealed the next day, after he had secured a fiancée, but he had wanted to come clean to the town and the people he had gotten to know in it, himself. But the cameras were here now, and he was full in their sights. Instinctively he turned his back on them. If only he could disappear, it would buy him a little time. How could he hold them off, so that he could get away before they got a photo?

A glance over his shoulder told him they were coming his way, although they weren't having an easy time of it. If Luke didn't know better, he'd swear it was as if the Anders Point crowd was purposely making it tough for them to wade past. Then he saw Wilfred, who had his back to the men, casually stretch out his foot behind him. One of them tripped over it, while the other stumbled into Eldridge, who had mysteriously gotten right into his way. At the same time a clear path through the crowd leading to the swinging doors into the kitchen seemed to open up in front of Luke.

But before Luke could take a step that way, a third man with a camera burst through the swinging doors and came right at him. In the process, the guy jostled into Ellen Turner, who was still standing between Luke and Jimmy. And that was a big mistake.

Luke instinctively stepped in front of her, using his body as a shield to protect her. Before he could do anything else, he saw Jimmy throw himself at the guy. The impact took them both backward into the refreshment table, which crashed to the floor under them. A shower of punch sprayed the crowd. Luke, meanwhile, got Ellen to a safe corner.

A voice in his ear said, "Would you like us to get rid of them for you, Your Highness?"

It was Carl, flanked by the rest of the hockey team. "You *knew?*" Luke asked, incredulous.

"Hell, buddy, the whole town's known for a while," Carl told him. "We just didn't want to let on to you or Annah."

"Why not?"

Carl shrugged. "We figured you had your reasons. Plus we didn't want to lose you on the team. Especially after we found out you play a decent center."

Another crash sounded from across the room. Jimmy was taking on the other two photographers, who had gone rushing over, thinking Luke was in the melee.

"So you want us to take care of this for you?"

"Yeah, you'd better step in, before that guy kills somebody," Luke said.

"Who, Turner? He's just thanking you for looking after his woman," Carl said. "Now go look after your own."

With a look of thanks, Luke left bedlam behind him and slipped into the blackness outside.

Luke took off on foot, as he knew Annah would be. She had left some time ago, before all the commotion, so he wondered how far she had gotten. Not far, he found out, catching sight of her on the town common.

He had left the scene at the dance way behind him at the firehouse, its sounds swallowed up by the vastness of the dark ocean that murmured at the foot of the bluff, its warmth by the chill of the December night. Here on the common, Christmas lights strung around evergreens twinkled as they swayed in the brisk wind off the sea. In the distance the castle loomed, its tower lit up against the dark night. Annah was leaning back against one of the massive oak trees whose ancestors had presided over the spot for time untold, her face turned up to the starless sky.

She didn't even glance at Luke as he approached her. He stood next to her, trying to pull all that had happened that night into focus, wondering where to start.

He didn't know whether she spoke to him or to the night surrounding them. "Do you think it's possible to want something too much?" she asked quietly.

Her question hit a bull's-eye deep inside him. *Yes. You,* he thought. He pulled her wrap closer around her shoulders, then put his arms around her, drawing her into the circle of his warmth. "Sweetheart, it's all right to want things."

"Not things you can't have," she whispered, her voice so wistful it tore him up inside.

"Is that why you pretended you didn't want kids?"

"I thought I didn't anymore, after...after the divorce." She began shaking.

He pulled her closer. "I assumed that your exhusband just didn't want them. But I found out tonight that wasn't the case."

"No. We both wanted them. We started trying right

away. But after three years I wasn't…''

The raw pain in her voice cut him to the core. ''Ah, sweetheart,'' he said soothingly.

''I…I couldn't…''

He heard blame in her halting words. ''That doesn't mean it was your fault,'' he argued.

She gave a choking sound, a half laugh, half sob. ''Luke, how can you say that? You met his wife tonight. In less than five years, they have two kids and one on the way! It sure wasn't *his* fault.''

''But that doesn't mean it was yours, either! Maybe it was the combination of the two of you. Did you feel that true-love thing with him?''

Her not answering was all the answer he needed.

''So then he wasn't the man for you,'' he said bluntly.

''What are you trying to say, Luke?''

''This,'' he said. He lowered his lips to hers and gave her a long, deep kiss. He felt passion flare instantly to life inside himself, felt her smoldering response. With an effort, he dragged his lips away. ''I'm saying give me two months, and I'll get you pregnant.''

''Luke!'' she said, pulling back abruptly to look up at him.

''Give me *one*. I swear, Annah.'' The raw masculinity of his bold promise vibrated in the air between them, hypnotic, magnetic.

She spun away, half in exasperation, half to stop the weak part of her from taking him up on his offer.

And she knew just what that offer was going to be. Dear God, he was going to propose to her. Her prince was going to offer her half his kingdom—more, he was going to offer her his love, his life, his future.

His future.

"Annah," he said, coming up behind her, putting his hands on her shoulders gently. "It's time to take this to its natural conclusion."

Yes, it was. But it wasn't the one he thought it was. "Not until you know everything," she said, turning to face him. She swallowed and then began. "After I couldn't— After three years Jimmy talked me into going to the doctor. It was awful. I had all those hideous tests, and nothing showed up. Nothing. So naturally Jimmy wanted to try even harder. But I—"

"What, Annah?" Luke asked softly.

She swallowed and looked right into his eyes. "I couldn't," she said simply. "I just couldn't try anymore. I just couldn't bear another month of disappointment, of pain—not only mine, but his. Being told that nothing was wrong only made it worse. Because I knew something *was* wrong. I just knew it."

She gave a shaky sigh. "Jimmy was upset, of course. We had gotten married to start a family, and now I wouldn't even try. When he realized that I wasn't changing my mind, he finally left me."

Luke had a choice word to say at that, or so she guessed, because it wasn't in English. "It was for the best," she insisted. "I gave him a divorce, which left him free to find true love and have the family he's always wanted."

"It was for the best," Luke agreed quietly. "Because it left you to do the same."

She shook her head. "No," she said simply.

No, she wouldn't go through the pain of trying and failing again. No, she wouldn't lose another man's love because she couldn't have his babies. No, she wouldn't let him stake his future happiness on a bad risk like her.

"No, you don't love me?" His words were clipped, his expression wary.

Love him? She was doing this *because* she loved him. "That's not the point," she said.

"Then what is?"

"There's not going to be any family for me."

His frustration was obvious. "Please try to be logical, Annah," he said with feeling. It was probably as close to pleading as he had ever come in his life. "If they didn't find any reason—"

"Please try to understand, Luke. This is not about laboratory tests or scientific data," she told him. "I'm trying to tell you that I'm afraid I just can't have children."

"How can you say that, until we've—"

"Luke," she said as gently as she could. "I'm not going to try."

That stopped his protest cold. He didn't seem to know what to say.

"I—I'm sorry," she whispered. "I wish I could. But I can't. I just…can't."

Seeing him standing there, head bowed, was almost more than she could stand. Her resolve wavered, but it didn't fail her. "Maybe you should leave now," she said quietly.

"Yes," he answered finally. "I think that would be best."

Luke packed up his things that night and drove out to the very tip of Anders Point. The castle was the logical place for him to go. He had already arranged with Whit to use it, and now that his cover was blown, there was no reason not to do just that.

. His teammates had taken care of the paparazzi for him, but Luke didn't want to take any chances on their returning, so he sent for his bodyguard the next day. Wilfred and Eldridge appointed themselves lieutenants, patrolling the bottom of the castle road so that no intruders could get by unnoticed. The craggy walls of the bluff would stop an advance from any other direction. And the castle itself was a nearly impenetrable fortress.

Luke spent hours pacing its corridors, heartache his only companion. Life was cold and lonely for the exiled prince. It wasn't because he missed the cozy comfort of Annah's house—which he did. Or because he missed being a part of town life, sitting at her coffee counter each morning, going to the grocery store, playing hockey—which he did.

He missed Annah, missed her with a frigid ache that penetrated right to the bone. No matter what he did, he couldn't seem to shake the insidious chill that had crept over him. It numbed his senses and slowed down the functioning of his brain.

And that he had to remedy. The Firehouse Dance had come and gone, and he was not engaged as he had planned—and had promised. The jaws of his marriage deadline opened up before him as the council of elders breathed down his neck with regular transatlantic phone calls. Time sped as he languished, and in his darker moments the idea that he might actually lose his crown and the chance to serve the country he loved became a very real possibility.

As a cold, gray dawn intruded on his nightly vigil for the third time, he got out of the chair that he had slumped in and ran his hand over his face. He hadn't thought about shaving since he had left Annah's. There was no need to, now that everyone knew who he was. But today he went up to the bathroom and started lathering up his face. He had grown accustomed to seeing that face during the past weeks in Anders Point, and he decided that he was going to take it with him when he went back to the Constellation Isles. From now on, he wasn't going to forget that while he was Prince Lucas, a part of him would always be Luke Hansson. He had Annah to thank for that.

She had helped him uncover that part of himself, the man who took pleasure in the simple comforts of life, by sharing her life with him. While he had lived with her he had come to love cookies warm from the oven, nighttime strolls to nowhere in particular, sharing an afghan while watching a video, retreating to a quiet corner to read a book just for fun. When he had slowed down the pace, even the littlest things had meant something, like smelling her perfume as she leaned over to help him figure out a tough clue in the daily crossword puzzle. Like listening to her laughter as she talked to Julie or Drew on the phone. He could try to take that feeling back with him, too.

But he couldn't take her, and that made everything else fade to black. She wasn't the woman he wanted for his wife, she'd said, and had gone on to prove it. It was all wrapped up and tied with a bow, a neat gift of logic that was beyond his power to refute. How could he marry a woman who came right out and said she would not even *try* to bear his children? He could not.

But he needed a wife. If not Annah, then someone else, logic told him. But every time he tried to decide which someone else he should choose, wayward thoughts intruded like unwelcome guests. Thoughts of Annah cradling that baby in the store; of Annah trying to hide her pain at the pregnancy of her ex-husband's wife, a finger of blame pointed straight at her; of Annah showering all of her unspent love and care on every man, woman and child at the Point. She had sent him away, but surely her pain equaled his own. He found himself hurting for her, wondering if she would continue to weep each month for her disappointed hopes. For if she wouldn't marry the man she loved, surely she wouldn't marry another. While he—he was left with no choice but to marry a woman who was not his true love.

He wondered which of them was to be less envied.

Annah had lived alone for nearly five years, but she had never known what loneliness felt like until now.

Oh, and it was so much more than being lonely for the sound of another voice, of dinner table conversation, of the reverberation of other footsteps in the house. It was Luke she was desolate without, and she missed him on every level, every plane of existence. Missed the sight of his tousled hair when he pulled on a sweater, of his feet stretched out in front of the hearth, of his rare smile. The smell of his aftershave, the warmth of his touch, the taste of his kiss. With him gone, her life had become a vacuum; her only feeling, pain.

She couldn't believe how much it had hurt to look in his empty room for the first time, knowing that he had really left. Of course, she hadn't expected him to do otherwise, after she had turned him away. Still, a small, selfish part of her wished that she had let him ask her to marry him. But if he had, oh, she wondered if she would have loved him enough to turn him down! By stopping his proposal, she had done the right thing, the unselfish thing, the noble thing. But all that was a poor substitute for having him by her side.

She sat in the window seat in her living room and bundled herself up in the afghan, although no amount of layering could chase away the chill that resided deep inside her. Against the night sky she could see the castle off in the distance. Within its walls her prince had confined himself. He hadn't been seen in town for over a week, not since the night of the Firehouse Dance. The night, she reminded herself, that he had wanted to choose his bride. She hadn't helped him after all. She had just made a mess of things for him. She wondered what he was going to do now.

So did the rest of the world. She had stopped reading the paper, stopped listening to the news, because she was tired of all the speculation about who Prince Lucas would choose as his bride...and when, since now only days remained before the deadline when his title would be revoked if he had not wed.

The whole world was waiting, wondering. But she was the only one who had a clue as to what the man in the castle was going through right now. She was suffering right along with him.

And, noble deeds aside, she knew that his choosing another woman to be his bride would bring her anything but relief.

Shivering, she drew the afghan closer around her, lost in her pain, eyes closed to the frozen tears that stabbed from within. Behind her the fire in the hearth, starving for lack of attention, slowly died.

Luke roused himself from his chair in the castle library without enthusiasm. His deadline had dwindled to days, but all emotion had ebbed from him. The ugly truth was that if he couldn't marry the woman he loved, it didn't much matter who he married.

He wandered into the kitchen, where a forgotten fire still smoldered. In the darkness it drew his gaze as the only point of light, feeble though it was. As he watched the glowing embers, a spark suddenly flew out, a radiant, irrepressible messenger that spoke to Luke more clearly than any words ever had.

He stood bolt upright. What had he been thinking? More importantly, *why* had he been thinking? In that flash point of insight, logic dimmed. Everything was clearly illuminated now, including the path that he must take.

It led him out of the door of the castle and into the waiting night.

Annah must have fallen asleep, because in the midst of her misery she was overtaken by a wonderful feeling that must have been a dream. What else could explain the way she suddenly became wrapped in a familiar warmth which brought her senses to life? Rising from the depths of sleep, she tried to identify the scent that went with it. Protective, exciting, masculine.

Luke. She was dreaming of having Luke near her again, because the only time she had ever felt this intoxicating warmth was around him. She clung fiercely to sleep so that the feeling might not end. If she couldn't have him in real life, she would have him in her dreams. Nevertheless she was drawn ever steadily into wakefulness until at last her eyes fluttered open.

He was there, kneeling next to her, watching her. Not a dream, not a fairy-tale prince, but a real man, the man Annah would love as long as her heart beat in her chest. The man she had loved so much, that she'd let him go.

"Hello," he said softly.

"What...Luke, what are you doing here?" she asked.

"I left something that belongs to me here. I came back to get it."

"But—" she began. She had cleaned his room, and he hadn't left a thing. Not a scrap, not a trace—nothing of his remained that she could save and keep hold of.

"Come over here," he said, helping her up. "Sweetheart, you're freezing." He led her over to the fireplace and sat her down on a floor pillow, arranging the afghan around her. Then he began tending the fire.

With patience and care and whispered words in a faraway tongue, he coaxed the dying embers back to life. Soon a renewed flame licked around the log he put on, and light and heat touched his skin and Annah's.

She watched him, brimming with the feelings that crowded within her. "Luke," she said. "Have you figured out what you're going to do?"

He turned to look at her, his gray eyes dark with feeling. "Yes. Now I know what I have to do, Annah. It all became clear to me, because of you."

"Me?"

He smiled at her surprise. "You. You're the one who taught me to trust my feelings. It took a long time to get here, but everything I went through was worth it."

He sat next to her, gazing at the fire. "It's all there, Annah. Just like you said. The spark of attraction, the steady glow of compatibility, the blaze of a spiritual passion. Once you find that, life is pretty damn cold and dark without it. That's not the way I intend to live my life. Or let the woman I love live hers.''

Annah's heart started beating faster. She couldn't speak.

He went on. "It's hard not to trust your feelings, when they're stronger than any force you've ever felt. You know what I'm talking about, don't you, Annah?''

Her chin started to tremble.

"It's okay, sweetheart," he said, cupping it in his hand. "I know it's scary. It was for me, too. But not anymore. So I'll go first.''

He gathered her into his arms and tipped her chin up to look right into her eyes. "I love you, Annah. I love you so much that I can't live without you. I want you to be my wife so that we can be together, where we belong, all the days of our lives.'' His voice broke, and he ended by whispering, "Please say you will.''

Tears leaked from the corners of her eyes. "But, Luke, I'm not the woman for you.''

"Yes, you are," he said gently. "Emotionally, physically, spiritually and every other way. This love of ours is meant to be. I can *feel* it.''

"But what if I won't—''

"All you have to do is love me.''

"But—''

"Just love me, Annah, and let me love you, and trust that everything else will work out.''

How could she, for his sake? "Luke, it's not just the succession. You want children so badly.''

"So do you," he said quietly.

She almost choked on the tightness in her throat. "I...I love you too much to let you jeopardize your dream.''

"And I love you too much to let you give up on

yours," he said. "Marry me and let me show you how to trade your fears for faith."

Annah blinked back her tears to look at him. He was watching her, waiting, but confident. It was a revelation for her. She had wanted to teach the jaded prince something about true love, but here he was teaching her something in return. That true love isn't an ending, but a beginning, the beginning of a new life together. That it engenders hope, optimism and the ability to rise above the pain of the past.

But could she do that? She didn't know. "Luke, I…I don't want to make you any promises that I can't keep."

"I understand," he said quietly, and he did. He could feel it, too, both her fear and, stronger, her secret yearning. That told him all he needed to know. "Annah, you don't have to make any promises. Your love is all I need."

She felt the last of her resistance melt away. Her fear was no match for the power of his unconditional love. Finally, she could stop fighting what her heart had been trying to tell her from the beginning.

"It's yours," she told him. Her love had been his all along. It belonged to him, and now that he had come to claim it, she would give it to him now and ever after.

She could feel his heart beating faster. "You'll be my wife?" he asked.

"Yes."

It was a short, sweet answer, but all that he needed. He followed it up with a long, sweet kiss. Wrapped in the warmth of his love, a new feeling bloomed in Annah, strong and vital. She realized that she was not afraid to try having babies with Luke, because he would love her no matter what the outcome. His love would either cushion the pain or multiply the joy. His love was all she needed, too.

She started to tell him, but he captured her mouth in another passionate kiss. It was just as well, she thought. She would wait until the night of their marriage to let him know.

All in all, she couldn't think of a better wedding gift to give the man she loved.

Epilogue

They were married in a matter of days, though Luke made sure that their honeymoon trip was a matter of weeks. And it was a matter of months before the nuptial celebrations that took them to every corner of the Constellation Isles ended, and the prince's new bride was finally settled in at his palace in the capital.

In the summer Annah and Luke found themselves back in Anders Point, Maine. But they weren't the only royal couple in town. Annah's friend Drew was now living in the castle at the tip of the Point with her husband, Prince Whit, and their daughter Lexi, who had just turned seven. And Whit's brother Erik was visiting from Isle Anders with his bride Julie and their baby son, Prince Nicholas, who took very well to being the center of attention. He went sweetly from arm to loving arm, all under the supervision of Lexi, who declared that she was adopting him as her baby brother until her own arrived at the end of the year.

Annah enjoyed every minute of the reunion. She liked seeing Luke buddying around with Erik and Whit, relaxed and smiling. Her husband had mellowed since his friends had first sent him to her and was enjoying more of life than he had before. When he held her close at night, he said it was because he had been reborn when he had first walked through her door.

If he had, then so had she. She knew she had never been happier.

She had remained close to Drew and Julie despite their new marriages and distant homes, but it was wonderful to be in the same place with them again, and the three friends slipped off together for long talks by the ocean. But after a while they always gravitated back to their families. Invariably the whole group would end up in the castle's big kitchen at the end of the day.

Annah looked around her at the roomful of people she loved. She saw Julie watching with love in her eyes as Erik gave his delighted baby boy tiny buzzing kisses on the tummy. And she caught Drew wiping a tear from the corner of her eye as Lexi threw her arms around Whit's neck and said, "I love you, Daddy." Love seemed to shine in every corner of the room, all around Annah.

And deep inside her, there was a tiny kernel of warmth that had never been there before. She had hugged the secret wonder of their unborn child to herself, but tonight—tonight she would share it with the man who stood across the room, his handsome face aglow as he watched his friends with their children. Her happiness increased as she anticipated Luke's joy when she told him her news.

Then he looked at her and smiled. And she knew that no matter what the future held for them, he couldn't love her any more than he did right now.

* * * * *

MEN at WORK
All work and no play? Not these men!

April 1998

KNIGHT SPARKS by Mary Lynn Baxter

Sexy lawman Rance Knight made a career of arresting the bad guys. Somehow, though, he thought policewoman Carly Mitchum was framed. Once they'd uncovered the truth, could Rance let Carly go...or would he make a citizen's arrest?

May 1998

HOODWINKED by Diana Palmer

CEO Jake Edwards donned coveralls and went undercover as a mechanic to find the saboteur in his company. Nothing—or no one—would distract him, not even beautiful secretary Maureen Harris. Jake had to catch the thief—*and* the woman who'd stolen his heart!

June 1998

DEFYING GRAVITY by Rachel Lee

Tim O'Shaughnessy and his business partner, Liz Pennington, had always been close—but never *this* close. As the danger of their assignment escalated, so did their passion. When the job was over, could they ever go back to business as usual?

MEN AT WORK™

Available at your favorite retail outlet!

 HARLEQUIN®   Silhouette®

Look us up on-line at: http://www.romance.net   PMAW1

BEVERLY BARTON

Continues the twelve-book series— 36 Hours—in April 1998 with Book Ten

NINE MONTHS

Paige Summers couldn't have been more shocked when she learned that the man with whom she had spent one passionate, stormy night was none other than her arrogant new boss! And just because he was the father of her unborn baby didn't give him the right to claim her as his wife. Especially when he wasn't offering the one thing she wanted: his heart.

For Jared and Paige and *all* the residents of Grand Springs, Colorado, the storm-induced blackout was just the beginning of 36 Hours that changed *everything!* You won't want to miss a single book.

Available at your favorite retail outlet.

Silhouette ®

Under the big sky, three unsuspecting couples
are granted their

BEST-KEPT WISHES

In this heartwarming new miniseries by Carol Grace,
three high school friends reveal their dreams on one starry
night. Now they're all grown up and about to discover their
dearest wishes can come true—with the help of love....

GRANTED: BIG SKY GROOM (#1277, February 1998)
Tally James longed for a ranch of her own—and wealthy rancher
Jed Whitmore owned the spread of her dreams. But would a marriage of
convenience to the groom who could fulfill all her wishes bring her
heartache—or love?

GRANTED: WILD WEST BRIDE (#1303, June 1998)
Rugged Josh Gentry had just about given up on happily-ever-after when
beautiful Bridget McCloud showed up on his ranch, cozying up to his little boy
and kissing this single daddy till his soul caught on fire. Could this pretty city
slicker be the bride this cowboy was looking for?

And look for Suzy Fenton's story, the exciting conclusion to this irresistible
series, coming in late 1998, only from Silhouette Romance!

Available at your favorite retail outlet.

Silhouette ROMANCE™

Look us up on-line at: http://www.romance.net   SRBKWJ-J

DIANA PALMER
ANN MAJOR
SUSAN MALLERY

RETURN TO WHITEHORN

In **April 1998** get ready to catch the bouquet. Join in the excitement as these bestselling authors lead us down the aisle with three heartwarming tales of love and matrimony in Big Sky country.

A very engaged lady is having second thoughts about her intended; a pregnant librarian is wooed by the town bad boy; a cowgirl meets up with her first love. Which Maverick will be the next one to get hitched?

Available in **April 1998**.

Silhouette's beloved **MONTANA MAVERICKS** returns in Special Edition and Harlequin Historicals starting in February 1998, with brand-new stories from your favorite authors.

Round up these great new stories at your favorite retail outlet.

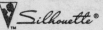